THE WALNUT TREE

John Cannell

The Author

John Cannell, a Chartered Engineer and Fellow of the Institution of Mechanical Engineers, was an aeronautical engineer during his early life – an aerodynamicist with Vickers-Armstrongs (Aircraft) Limited working on such classic aircraft as the VC10, the BAC 1-11 and TSR-2. With the demise of the aircraft industry, following cuts by successive governments at the time, he migrated to building services and worked for international firms of consulting engineers and finally the University of Cambridge.

During all that time his enduring interest was in writing, but it was only on retirement that he found the time not only to help out as an Essex Wildlife Trust volunteer at Warley Place but also to fulfil his ambition and write a novel. That novel was *The Wall* and it was well enough received to merit a sequel – *The Walnut Tree*.

With his limited knowledge of botany neither book would have been possible without the help of the other volunteers at Warley Place, who were only too ready with help whenever he needed it.

Author's Note

When I was writing *The Wall* I thought it would be a little one-off tale that would sell well enough to make a small amount of money for Essex Wildlife Trust and, once finished, I could concentrate on helping out at Warley Place and sorting out the archives. To my delight the book was well received and sold better than I expected; it was with mixed feelings, however, that I found I was frequently being asked when the sequel was coming out. Well here it is.

As before, the story alternates between two time frames, 1920 (having moved on a year since *The Wall*) and the current day. Ellen Willmott of course continues to play a big part as does Jacob Maurer, her highly respected alpine gardener, who is remembered for being a true gentleman as well as for his horticultural skills.

Current events and the individuals named in this period are, as before, fictitious, but the tenor of life at Warley Place is pretty much as described – good humoured and hard working, concerned only with the stewardship of Warley Place for Essex Wildlife Trust.

To readers who have not visited Warley Place it is worth noting that it is a nature reserve, not a garden or a park, even though the spring flowers are incredibly beautiful and exotic trees and shrubs abound. There is no gift shop; there are no toilets, and only a bare minimum of way markers. That is why the general public are not encouraged to visit other than on organised public days, although Essex Wildlife Trust members are welcome at any time.

I don't know whether to thank those who nagged me into writing a second book or not. I suppose I should. I'll think about it. My thanks certainly go to my brother Derek who read the initial draft very thoroughly, found countless typos and other errors, pointed them out with great tact, and made suggestions for improvement. Also my wife Shirley and my good friend Chris Darby, Fiona Agassiz and Ailsa Wildig who put up with me at Warley Place, and Jacob Maurer's granddaughter Trish Kilpatrick, all of whom made valuable comments and gave encouragement when I needed it. Kate Portman gave me advice

3

about Spetchley Park without which I could not have written that particular chapter. Many other people helped in different ways, but since authors' notes don't usually get read I hope they will understand if I don't list them all.

My knowledge of the German language is negligible and I mentioned to my friend Martina Hoge-Lees that I was looking for a phrase for the German officer to speak in the first chapter when faced with a gesture from his English counterpart. Something like 'An end to the senseless killing' I suggested. She said that her grandfather wrote those very words, 'Schluss mit dem sinnlosen Morden,' many times when he sent letters back from the German trenches in that awful war. It touched me deeply.

One unexpected benefit of *The Wall* was that it established contact with Jacob Maurer's grandchildren and with his daughter Iris, the latter now living in America. As well as being delightful people, they also provided interesting and useful background material.

I would therefore like to dedicate this book to a man I would dearly love to have known – Jacob Maurer.

THE WALNUT TREE

John Cannell

Printed and bound in the UK by Biddles Limited, Kings' Lynn,
Norfolk
ISBN 978-0-9556449-1-7

1

Dearest Ken,

It's strange how things happen all through our lives. Sometimes they turn out well, sometimes they don't. I could easily have never met you and continued my dreary life not thinking about what might have been.

A mortar round burst just in front of the trench. Alfie ducked involuntarily and one of his feet slipped off the duckboard into the sludge below as mud showered over him. Cursing, he slowly pulled his leg out of the slime that would suck a wounded man to his death given half a chance. An awful end, Alfie thought as he wiped his filthy hands on his equally filthy greatcoat and shook the worst of the sticky mess off his boot.

'All right Alfie?'

'Aye Bert.'

His pal turned back to the periscope with its view over the sandbags, watching for any movement in no man's land. The opposing positions were only a couple of hundred yards apart, separated by barbed wire and shell holes; shell holes full of watery slime in which many a man had drowned and even the rats avoided. Past the German line were the remains of a chateau, thought now to be a command post of some sort. The upper floors were just stumps of walls, the result of years of bombardment, and the lower floor must surely soon collapse under the weight of the rubble above it, despite its reinforcement.

'They reckon it'll all be over soon,' continued Bert. 'Then it's back to Blighty for us. We'll see 1919 after all.'

There was a loud crack close by then a crump further away as the German mortar was given a predictable reply.

'Fat chance.'

'No, sarge says it's true this time. Probably tomorrow.'

'So I heard. Like I say, fat chance. Just look over there. Does Fritz look finished to you?'

'No, he don't,' agreed Bert, somewhat reluctantly.

'I seen some prisoners yesterday,' said Alfie. 'I seen a lot since I've been here. And you know what? Take their uniforms off and they look just like us. I bet they've got kids like we have, wives like we have. Probably as poor as we are too.'

'Alfie, quiet,' said Bert, looking about. 'You know they don't like that sort of talk. What'll you do when you go back? Will your old job be open for you? Gardening, wasn't it, for some old bat in Essex?'

'I don't know about her being an old bat. She's a bit eccentric, that's for sure, but anyway I didn't really work for her, I worked for a bloke from Switzerland. He's a gent, been there years; looks after her alpine garden. Yes, I'd like to go back and Jacob – the Swiss chap – has written a few times and tells me my old job's waiting for me. What about you?'

'Dunno. Dodging bullets, that's all I'm good for, and when I'm not doing that then sitting in a cold wet trench picking lice off meself. Not much call for that skill in civvy street, is there?'

'All right men?'

Alfie turned to see Lieutenant Martinsyde crouching behind him.

'Fine thanks sir. All quiet. Hope it stays that way.'

'May be some action in the morning.'

'What?' cried the two soldiers in dismay. 'We'd heard rumours that it was going to be over soon.'

'Maybe. But we need to get that post, and to get that we need to take those trenches. The sergeant will fill you in later. Wonder what Fritz is doing?'

He started to stand, to see over the parapet, only to get grabbed and hauled down by Alfie as a bullet thudded into the back wall.

'Sorry sir. Sniper's got our range. He's had a go several times.'

'Thank-you Hedges. I owe you one. Good meal tomorrow, I believe. Barnes has purloined some chickens. God knows where he gets these things. I don't think I want to know. He makes a damn good mess orderly though.'

He went off at a crouch, shaking his head.

'Wally Barnes is a friend of yours, ain't he Alfie?'

'No, not a friend,' said Alfie, his face tight. 'He just comes from the same town as me. He might be good at thieving, but he's sod all use at fighting. Have you ever seen him up front here?'

8

Wally Barnes was indeed good at keeping them fed and in fact managing to get a few other things like cigarettes and the occasional bottle of wine. If what the troops got was anything to go by, God knows what he passed on to the officers. Alfie reckoned he did it to make sure he stayed out of the trenches. Must have a flair for that sort of thing though. He took care of the blokes' personal things when they copped it, to send them back home. Alfie wasn't alone in wondering how much really did get sent home and how much got mislaid on the way. No one said anything though, not while Wally kept them happy.

Alfie glanced at his friend.

'I'll take over now Bert, you get some rest. It's going to be a long night.'

His friend nodded his thanks, wrapped his greatcoat round himself, adjusted his pack and settled down in a niche in the trench wall.

Alfie hardly dared to think about it; the prospect of getting back to his wife and children; not having to wonder if each day would be his last; sleeping in a real bed at night, and not having to pick lice off himself morning noon and night.

The quiet nights were the worst in one way; it was too easy to drift off to sleep. They all had various ways of keeping themselves awake. He often imagined Ellen Willmott suddenly appearing and catching him not working and giving him an earful, or Jacob quizzing him about the names of the flowers.

He was always happy, was Jacob. Losing his wife, Rosina, just after her having their ninth kid, that must have been a real blow. He liked writing letters back to his sisters in Switzerland in the evening; he'd told Alfie that once. In German, they were. Must have been tricky that. They could have thought he was a spy. Mind you, the old girl would have sorted them out if anyone came out with anything like that. Real clever, he was, knowing all those languages. French too, apparently. Perhaps that was the secret of being happy; learn a language and write letters. No, Alfie thought, he had enough trouble with English.

'You still on watch Hedges?'

He jumped. He hadn't heard the sergeant approach.

'Yes sarge. Bert told me to wake him but he's in such a fine deep sleep I thought I'd let him have an extra few minutes. I'm not tired.'

'You will be tomorrow,' said Sergeant Miller, digging Bert with his foot. 'Get some sleep, that's an order.'

'Sorry Alfie,' said Bert, stretching and yawning. 'You should have woken me. Go on, I've warmed the bed for you.'

Alfie eased himself down as their sergeant disappeared round the bend in the trench, dug in a zigzag to avoid a burst sending shrapnel along the whole of its length. He shut his eyes and imagined himself walking from the chestnut trees down to the gorge, looking at each tree in turn. He just made it to the Persian ironwood tree. He rarely made it any further, however wide awake he thought he was.

'Hey, Alfie, heard the latest? It's over, Alfie, it's over.'

Alfie forced himself from his fitful sleep and rubbed his eyes at the dawn light.

'What's over?'

'The war. Alfie, we've made it.'

'Come on Bert, how many bloody times have we heard that?'

'No, sarge told me. Some time this morning, or p'raps this afternoon.'

'Yeah, or p'raps next week, or next month. Next year even. The lieutenant told us last night it's action this morning, remember?'

'No, this time it's true.'

'If it's bloody true, why is sarge looking so bleedin' angry then?'

Bert whirled round to look behind him to see their sergeant, Ernie Miller, coming towards them at a crouch. His eyes were blazing, a deep furrow between his lowered eyebrows.

'One last job lads,' he growled. 'Get ready, we move in fifteen minutes.'

'Sarge?' Bert could hardly speak, his jaw had dropped so far. 'We'd heard it's over.'

'Well whatever you heard, Major bloody Winter has other ideas. Fritz needs to be cleared out and we've got to do it.'

'But they haven't shelled them yet,' said Alfie.

'No, and they're not going to. We are to surprise them.' The sarcasm dripped from his mouth.

'Oh, right sarge,' said Alfie. 'Two hundred yards of open ground full of mud and shell holes, barbed wire in front of their lines, and we surprise them? Yeah, we'll do that all right. A Christmas present for their machine guns, once they've stopped laughing, only it's November, not the twenty fifth of bloody December.'

'All right Hedges, I don't like it any more than you do and neither does the Lieutenant, but the war is still on and we do what we're told.'

'Can't we just sit tight for a bit?' asked Bert. 'If it's right about the end coming then – '

The sergeant didn't even bother to reply.

Alfie's brow creased. 'So the whole battalion is going to risk being slaughtered – for what?'

'Not the whole battalion lad, just our platoon. It's a very local objective, but apparently important.'

Alfie shook his head in wonder. About as important as the mud they'd fought over for the past four years, he thought.

'Just one thing,' said Sergeant Miller. 'The lieutenant has said whatever happens, just follow him. And no one is to fire until he does or unless they start shooting first. Hold your rifle at the port. Got that?'

'Yes sarge,' they muttered in unison.

'Fifty men,' said Bert when their sergeant had gone. 'Just a platoon against a machine gun and a trench full of Fritz, and our arms at the port. What are they playing at?'

'Dunno. I s'pose they know what they're doing.'

'They don't seem to have ever since this lot started,' replied Bert.

After a moment's silence they started checking their gear. Rifles first, mechanism clear, magazine full, bayonet fixed. Spare ammo; mills bombs; helmet straps done up; boot laces tight.

'I feel sick Alfie,' whispered Bert.

'Me too. What a time to go, right when it's almost over.'

All too soon they heard the whistle and dutifully clambered over the top, rifles held across their bodies.

11

It was eerily quiet. The sandbags in front of the enemy trenches were visible through the mist behind the barbed wire. They knew the way through their own wire, but it had been marked the night before just in case. In between the two lines was a scene from the moon. Craters, abandoned equipment, and mud.

The lieutenant led the way, walking much more slowly than usual. Alfie noticed that he wasn't holding his revolver. Strange that.

It seemed to take forever. Feet slipping in the mud, Alfie stepped to the right round a shell hole, keeping well clear of the edge. He didn't feel sick any more. Too frightened to feel anything.

He could make out the machine gun and the figures hunched over it and flinched, waiting for the flashes from the muzzle. He hoped it would be quick, trying not to think about a lump of lead tearing its way through his flesh. If he flung himself down and pretended to be shot he soon would be when the rescue party found he wasn't injured. A flesh wound perhaps, and hope it didn't get infected? A lot of his mates had died from flesh wounds. God this was stupid. Please get it over with.

The lieutenant put up his arm for them to stop. What the hell was he doing? Giving Fritz an easy target? But he was walking forward on his own, revolver still in its leather holster.

'No more killing,' he said.

A figure rose from the German trench and made its way through the wire, also unarmed.

'Schluss mit dem sinnlosen Morden,' the enemy officer agreed. 'An end to this senseless killing. We have lost. It will all be over in a few minutes I believe.'

'We have both lost,' said the lieutenant. 'The whole world has lost.'

They saluted each other.

Alfie threw down his rifle and sank to his knees, turning his face away so that his friend would not see his tears. For the first time he could think about the future. His wife Bessie, the two children he had hardly seen and who wouldn't know who he was, and his job in the gardens. So many of his mates wouldn't have that; so many of his mates were dead.

It was almost eleven in the morning on the eleventh day of November. The year was nineteen eighteen.

2

I'll never forget how kind you were that time when we first met. Silly, I know, but I've always been frightened by new places and new faces. I was really looking forward to Warley Place and when I got there I was so scared I almost turned round and went home again. I really am stupid.

Elsie was wearing her best blouse, a yellow one she'd got from the Oxfam shop in the High Street, a light blue jacket that was rather washed out, although the pastel shade disguised that a bit, and a flowery skirt. That was from Cancer Research. Her long black hair looked nice over the yellow blouse and blue jacket, she knew that, but the skirt didn't really match. Her other one was very shabby looking though, she couldn't have worn that. Now she wished she'd put her jeans on, like most of the other women walking up the wide path from the road. Well, not most of them, but a lot of them. None of them had yellow blouses, either, they had anoraks and jumpers. She'd thought it would go with the flowers, but she couldn't see any daffodils and the crocuses were mostly purple. Now everyone would be looking at her, knowing that she didn't know when daffodils would be out. They all looked so clever. They'd probably know the names of all the trees as well as the flowers; Latin names too, she wouldn't wonder.

The bit in the paper had said that anyone who was interested in flowers should go to one of the public days at Warley Place. It was a bit muddy when it was wet, one of her friends had told her, but on a bright sunny day like today it was supposed to be wonderful.

Getting here was a bit of a drag. There was a bus, but it didn't run very often and she hadn't found out when that was. She didn't mind walking, even if it was a bit further than she'd thought, and she'd had the sense to wear comfortable shoes.

Hesitating at the wide gate leading to an equally wide path, she plucked up courage and stepped in. Stopping after only a few yards, she turned to look at the lovely little cottage on her left. It looked as if it was made of wood. Wooden walls, and even the roof slates from the look of them. It seemed a bit dilapidated, but it was the sort of place she'd sometimes dreamed about getting if she ever got married. Not that she was likely to marry anyone who could afford anything like that.

She jumped and hopped on to the grass verge as a car apologetically peeped its horn at her.

'Sorry,' smiled a middle-aged man as he drove slowly past, she assumed to a car park somewhere further on.

A big 4x4 followed the previous car and the driver slowed down and looked at her as he passed. She smiled at him, but he just stared at her feet before driving on. She looked down and felt her face heat up as she saw the little blue flowers on which she was standing. Quickly stepping off them she hoped that the next group of visitors walking in through the gate hadn't noticed.

'Lovely day isn't it?' a good-looking young man, casually dressed in a green jumper and jeans, said cheerfully.

'It is,' she responded, a smile automatically coming to her face, and she turned to follow them. She was here, and she wasn't leaving until she had seen what it was all about.

She hoped the flowers had their names on labels stuck in the ground, like in the garden centres. She had a notebook, one of those with a little pencil in it, in her handbag, and she was going to write down the names of any rare plants so that on Tuesday after the holiday she could go in to work and casually mention what she had seen. They would laugh at her, but she knew that secretly they'd be impressed.

The path suddenly opened out as she walked on, and she saw a dozen or so cars parked in a small area on her left behind the cottage, a harassed-looking man trying to shoehorn more into spaces between the trees. To her relief she saw the splash of yellow on the meadow beyond the car park; daffodils were out after all.

There was another big gate in front of her across the path, and people milled about all over the place; they seemed to be drifting towards a strange tent that had open sides, just a roof on poles really. There was a little table in there and some people sitting behind it. Oh God, perhaps you had to pay to get in. She wondered how much she had in her purse; not much, she was certain of that, just the bus fare home, if she could find out when it came, and a bit in case she needed a drink or an ice cream. Not that there was anywhere to buy either of those things, she noticed.

There was a big notice board by a tree. It had a plan of the gardens and a picture of a woman on it, so she made her way to see if it said what the entrance fee was. Just as she reached it a family came over to look too and she was in their way. She moved aside, suddenly nervous, wondering now whether perhaps she should forget the idea and just go home. The sound of dozens of voices merged into one meaningless gabble, making her want to put her hands over her ears, and she began to panic. She couldn't focus on anything and didn't know which way to go. Carried along with the flow of the crowd, before she knew it they had all had gone past the strange tent and been squeezed through a small gate at the side, like toothpaste from a tube.

Once on the other side she stopped for a moment to gather herself together and someone bumped into her. Elsie mumbled an apology, feeling her face heat up again, and moved forwards. A woman at the front of the group started to speak loudly, telling them something about someone called Ellen Willmott.

Her heart was banging; she had to get away from them. There was a big field to her right; she couldn't go there, it would be too obvious, but there was a seat over to her left in front of some shrubs and she made for it across a strip of long grass, stumbling over a hidden drainage channel as she went. She'd pretend she'd got a stone in her shoe and sit down. Thank God she'd chosen the sandals instead of the high heels she'd first picked up.

It was really just a log split along its length, perched on top of two stumps, but she sank down on it, comforted by the solid varnished reliability, and wanted to cry. She swivelled her head away from the group that was continuing along the path, to look through the shrubs at the pond behind her.

Why had she come here? After reading about it in the local paper she'd told her friends at work that she was coming, now she wished she hadn't. Perhaps if she stayed for a few minutes, then walked back into Brentwood, she could honestly say she had been. But then they'd ask questions. What if one of them had been here too? Then they'd soon find out she hadn't walked round and they'd laugh at her. She was a grown woman, twenty years old and her whole life ahead of her. Why should she worry if the girls laughed at her? They already laughed at her being so thin. She supposed she was, really, but it was better than being too fat, wasn't it?

Getting ideas above her station, that was her problem, her father had told her. She loved flowers. Trees were good, stately some of them, majestic even, solid and dependable, but flowers were beautiful and delicate. She knew the names of a lot of them; daffodils, pansies, tulips, roses of course, they were easy, but she knew quite a few wild flowers too. She liked daisies, even buttercups and dandelions. She was looking out for a book on plants, but they didn't get handed in to the charity shops so much as stories. She'd like to work with flowers, but the pay wasn't very good and she hadn't had any experience.

One day she'd go to college and learn all about them, and people would ask her what was this flower? What was that one? She'd have to save up first though, and that was difficult, what with the money she gave her mother for her keep. It was far too much, but it wasn't her mother's fault. She knew a lot of it went to her father. She didn't want to know what that was for.

'Are you all right?'

She froze.

'Are you OK? Do you need any help?'

She slowly turned her head towards the voice.

It was the young man who had spoken to her by the gate when she had first come in. Dark hair, like hers, slim, wearing well-worn jeans, trainers and a green jumper with a few holes in it and a label saying 'Volunteer' pinned on his chest. And a beautiful friendly smile. Only a few years older than her, too, but out of her league, she could tell that immediately.

'I didn't mean to startle you.'

'I, er, I'm just getting a stone out of my sandals.'

Damn. She could see him looking at her eyes, and she knew they were like saucers. They always were when she was nervous.

'Can I help?'

'Oh, I mean I've just got it out.'

'Have you been here before?'

'No, never. My friends told me about it. In the office. I work in an office.'

It wasn't a lie, she told herself. She did work in an office. She cleaned it. But now he's going to ask what I do, she realised with horror, and then I'll have to lie. And she wasn't very good at lying, she knew that.

'Would you like to go round with that party?' He motioned to the group disappearing up the path.

She shook her head dumbly. He smiled.

'Well we can't have you wandering all alone, can we? Come on, I'll give you a personal guided tour. I'm on my own and I could do with the company.'

'But I thought you were with those other people when you came in?'

'Well yes, they were some friends. They've just come to walk round, but I've come to help out if I can. I'm a volunteer with the Essex Wildlife Trust.' He looked back at the gazebo. 'Actually I haven't been a volunteer for very long and I'm scared stiff of having to take a group round. There will be at least one show-off who knows more than I do about the place and lets everyone know it. So you'd be saving my life.'

He turned so that she could follow him, but she couldn't get off the bench. All she could feel was her heart pounding against her ribs and the shaking of her hands.

'I'm sorry, I'm just being presumptuous,' he apologised. 'If you'd rather not....'

'No, please, if you've got the time that would be lovely,' she said falteringly. Her legs had gone weak. What would happen if she tried to get up?

He sat down beside her.

'You've said you haven't been here before, but do you know anything about Warley Place?'

'Only a little,' she admitted. 'The Essex Wildlife Trust looks after it, and someone called Ellen Willmott used to own it. Oh, and there are lots of lovely flowers here, especially in the spring. And I love flowers. That's why I'm here.'

Her heart was beginning to slow down now; she could only just feel it pulsating quietly in her chest.

'That's a lovely reason for coming,' he smiled. 'Yes, Ellen Willmott used to own it. She was a very rich lady and she used her money to make what many thought was one of the finest

18

gardens in England. She got plants from all over the world. No expense was spared. She finally ran out of money and when she died the place fell apart. The house was demolished and the sycamores and weeds grew so fast it all turned into a jungle. The Essex Wildlife Trust maintains it as a wildlife refuge, but also tries to keep it looking beautiful in her memory.'

'She must have been a wonderful woman.'

'She was,' he agreed. 'She got a bit crabby in her old age apparently, but still wonderful. She died a few years before the last World War, in 1934.'

'I saw her picture on that board by the gate. She was beautiful.'

'When she was young, yes,' he said. 'And so are you.'

'No I'm not,' she said, reddening but savouring his words. 'I'm a skinny nobody. She was a beautiful somebody.'

'You are somebody,' he said. 'I don't know who yet, but I'll find out. I'm Kenneth, by the way. Ken.'

She took the hand held out to help her to her feet, vastly reassured by the slight flush that now covered his own face. His hand was that of someone who worked outside, she was relieved to find. Tough, but not harsh. He wouldn't notice that hers was not that of a pampered office worker. Thank goodness she always wore her rubber gloves when she was working.

'I'm Elsie,' she said, relieved to find that she hadn't fallen over. 'Elsie Clark.'

They started to walk back over the grass towards the path.

'And thanks for not saying that's a lovely name,' she said, surprised at her own boldness.

'There's nothing wrong with it,' he assured her.

He'd let go of her hand now. She knew he had to but hoped he'd take it again later on. Perhaps if she tripped!

'Before we go on,' she said. 'Who lives in that lovely little cottage by the gate?'

'I don't know. It's not part of Warley Place that the Wildlife Trust manages, I think it's leased to someone else. It used to be where one of the gardeners lived in Ellen Willmott's time though; Jacob Maurer. He looked after the alpine garden. At one time he, his wife and nine children lived there!'

'Bloody 'ell!'

19

She felt herself heating up again. Oh well, that's blown it, he'll be off with someone a bit more ladylike now. But he was laughing.

'One of my favourite expressions,' he said. 'It sums things up so succinctly.'

'No, I –'

But he was standing very still, listening intently.

'Hear that?' he asked, looking up at the trees behind them.

'Hear what?'

'The bird. That sort of trilling sound.'

'I do,' she said. 'It's a pretty sound. What is it?'

'I think it's a nuthatch. I'm not very good at birds so I could be wrong. Look, there it is.'

She saw it, quite close, on a trunk. Darkish grey on the upper side, light colour underneath.

'See the dark streak on the head, across its eyes,' he whispered.

'Oh yes.'

'I wonder if... Damn. Oh well, I was hoping to see it walk down the tree.'

'Why?'

'Well sometimes they come down head first. Woodpeckers can't do that, nor can treecreepers. I've never seen one do it though, I was hoping today would be the day.'

'Well I've never seen a nuthatch at all,' she said, 'so it's something for me to remember.'

As they stood there they looked across the path at the meadow that stretched between the garden and the main road down which she had walked.

'That used to be covered in crocuses,' he said. 'There's still quite a few, as you can see, but nothing like what it was fifteen or twenty years ago.'

'There's a lot under that tree though,' she said, pointing to a riot of colour round a big tree just by the edge of the path.

'Come on then, let's go over and have a look.'

'Why is there a fence round it?' she asked as they crossed the path and drew closer.

'Rabbits,' he explained. 'A few years ago hardly any flowers came up and we wondered if the rabbits got in there and ate the nice tender shoots as they sprouted. When we put the fence there things improved and they've got better and better each year. Actually some people say it might not be rabbits, it might be deer.'

'It's beautiful,' she murmured. 'I'm so glad I came.'

'We've only just started,' he said, smiling at her pleasure and turning to continue the tour.

'It's a big path,' she said as they waited for another group to pass through, more for something to say than because she'd really thought about it. It was quite wide, probably a couple of metres across she guessed, made mostly of pebbles, raised in the middle and lower at the edges. Further on, where it disappeared into the trees, she could see it was edged with logs cut in half along their length, tiles wedged behind them to stop the dirt spilling through from the banks either side.

'That's because it isn't really a path,' he said. 'Well it is now, but it used to be more than that. It was the main road to Brentwood until that was diverted to where it is now. That was in eighteen sixty-six, just over ten years before the Willmotts arrived. This then became the carriageway to the house, so it's very old. Just imagine whose feet walked along it in days gone by.'

She tried to imagine, but shook her head. 'I can't,' she said. 'I just can't imagine what it was like in those days. But then I was never very good at history at school.'

Oh please don't ask what school I went to, she pleaded silently. Why didn't she think before she spoke?

'Me neither,' he laughed. 'They tell me the pilgrims on their way to Canterbury walked along it, but I haven't a clue when that was. Anyway, just imagine you are Ellen Willmott, sitting in your horse-drawn carriage, and I am driving you home having picked you up from Brentwood Station after your day out in London.'

She laughed too, delighted at the thought.

'And,' she said, 'I have got down from my carriage to look at my flowers more closely.'

'And I am the head gardener,' he said, 'showing them to you. But you must promise not to tell me off if you see any weeds!'

'I promise. But I thought you were the driver?'

'Just a job I do on the side to make up my money.'

'Are you saying I don't pay you enough?'

He laughed. She felt a thrill that she hadn't felt for a long time. Not ever, in fact, not that she could remember.

The ground at each side of the drive banked upwards, and each bank was a mass of colour. Crocuses, mostly, but many she didn't recognize. But one near her was familiar.

'Oh look,' she said. 'A snowdrop. I thought they'd all be gone by now.'

'Yes, they have mostly,' he agreed. 'But some hang on quite late. I don't know what that one is; they all look the same to me. Most of them are *Galanthus nivalis*.'

'Most of them are what?' she asked, immediately wanting to take the words back. Now he would think she was ignorant.

'It's the Latin name for the common snowdrop,' he explained.

'Gal-an-thus ni-va-lis' she spelled out. 'I'm sorry, I do like flowers but I don't know their other names.'

He patted his pockets.

'Sorry, I haven't got anything to write on or with, otherwise I'd have written it down for you.'

'I have,' she said eagerly, delving into her bag and pulling out the little notebook.

He took it from her and wrote 'Galanthus nivalis, the Common Snowdrop' in strong clear letters. 'Flowers in February, but can still sometimes be seen much later.' He passed the notebook back to her.

She imagined herself on Tuesday saying 'Oh, and I saw a Galanthus nivalis by the drive. It's very late for them.' But she knew she wouldn't. Her voice would tremble too much and they would laugh and it just wouldn't work.

'It's a good idea to keep a notebook,' he said. 'There is so much to see and you'll forget most of it by the time you get to the other end. Put down about the nuthatch, too.'

She flushed with pleasure and scribbled down what he had said earlier.

'Actually snowdrops are coming out earlier and earlier as the winters get warmer, and a lot are out in January,' he continued. 'In fact we've seen quite a few crocuses that early, too.'

They walked slowly up the drive.

'If you can come again a bit later the rhododendrons are a real sight,' he said, pointing at the buds with the colours showing through.

'I'd love that,' she said, sighing. Could this really be happening to her? She wished her mother could see how happy she was just now.

They walked slowly along the shady drive.

'See that tree,' Ken said, stopping suddenly. 'It was blown over in the gales in nineteen eighty-seven but some of the roots....'

Elsie's heart dropped. He was talking distractedly, as if he had something else on his mind. Was he bored with her already? He was looking back down the drive and as she followed his gaze she saw a blonde man of about Ken's age closely inspecting one of the rhododendrons.

'What's special about that rhododendron?' she asked. 'It's not even got flowers on it yet.'

'Nothing,' he said. 'Nothing at all.'

3

Whatever happens now, I'd like you to know what a difference you have made to me. I've never met anyone quite like you, and never will again. I still can't believe how much has happened in these few short weeks.

Alfie Hedges turned up the frayed collar of his jacket and trudged wearily down the drive in the fading light, past Jacob Maurer's little chalet and out through the gate of Warley Place. He looked down the road towards his own overcrowded cottage, a good walk from where he was standing, and then to his right at the *Thatchers Arms*, fingering the few coins in his pocket. She'd given him hell last time, but it had been a long day today and he was knackered. Just one would do no harm. What was there for him at home anyway? Just noise and a cold dinner.

An old nag appeared from round the bend in the road, plodding its way up the slope as it dragged a cart behind, loaded with logs for someone's fire. He saw the raindrops splashing in the puddles by the verge and pulled his cap tighter on his head. He turned towards home, then stopped, muttered 'bugger it' to himself and veered right towards the warm comfort of the pub. He paused for a moment, glancing at South Lodge. Jacob wasn't back yet but the sound of young children's laughter brought a pang of envy to the surface. Max, the eldest, had gone back to Switzerland for a bit. Shame really, Alfie had liked his mischievous humour. Even so, eight of them left, plus Jacob and his cousin Friedi to look after them, all in that small cottage – and still they laughed? He was glad for Jacob. Envious, yes, but glad. He turned back to the pub door and went in.

'Usual Alfie?'

'Aye.'

He sat down at an empty table, not wanting company this evening. His stomach hurt, his knees were stiff and he had a headache. He lifted the tankard to his lips.

Was this all there was to life? Hard work all day working in Willmott's garden from six in the morning till six at night, earache when he got home, screaming kids on Sundays wanting to go out when all he wanted to do was to stay in bed?

He thumped his tankard down and cursed as precious beer shot out over the table. He wiped it with his hand and sucked his wet fingers.

'Another bad day Alfie?'

He looked up.

'Wally.'

'Don't look too pleased to see me then, it might hurt.'

'Sorry Wally. Yes, a bad day. The bitch is late with the pay again and I've got the missus on my back and no more credit to get me food.'

'Too bad.'

'Bleedin' war's well gone now. All that time in the trenches and what's happened to us? Worse off than before, that's what. Them that stayed at home did all right though.'

'At least we got out alive,' Wally grunted.

'Yes,' agreed Alfie.

They sat in silence for a minute.

'Do you know, I miss it?' said Alfie.

'What? The freezing cold, the mud, the rats, getting shot at, never knowing if that day would be your last? Or killing Germans, that must be it.'

'No, not that. And if the truth were known I don't think I ever killed a German all the time I was there.'

'Come off it, you must have done.'

'No, I never aimed my rifle at anyone. I just fired over their heads. And thank God I was never in a position to have to bayonet one. No, it was the companionship. We was all in it together like. I hated it, but I miss it. And I can't stop thinking about all my mates that was killed. Remember Billy Bridges? He was blown up –'

'You're right Alfie,' Wally broke in. 'But we've got to make the best of things. No good thinking about the past. Like you said, them what stayed out of it did all right. They just got to pay us our dues.'

'And how do we make them do that?' asked Alfie. 'They've got plenty, true, but they're hanging on to it. Don't give a shit about us.' He glanced out of the window to the gate. 'She's got a packet, I know that. The old bat says she hasn't, but she must have. She's one of them what keeps it to herself. She's got enough to look after the royals when they visit, but not enough to pay us poor buggers a living wage and we can't even get that out of her on time.'

His companion looked about through half-closed eyes before speaking. Jacob Maurer, Ellen Willmott's loyal alpine gardener of many years, never set foot in the pub, but some of the other gardeners did.

'She's certainly got you suckers working your pants off. There used to be ten times as many looking after that place. You told me that.' He nodded in the direction of the house. 'She don't pay you ten times as much for doing the same work though, does she?'

'Too true she don't.'

He contemplated the bottom of his now empty jug. He knew that in fact they weren't paid a bad wage, not compared with some. But Ellen Willmott had about a hundred gardeners working for her once, now there were not much more than a handful to keep the estate in some sort of order. They had to deal with her other properties too. Wellmead, the big house over the other side of the road with its fourteen acres of gardens, was a nightmare on its own, what with all those roses, as well as the grass and the wild flowers and trees, all needing attention. Then there was the farm too. They just couldn't keep up.

'How's the missus?' his companion asked eventually.

Alfie shrugged. 'Another on the way,' he said.

'Dunno how you can afford it.'

'Can't.'

'Refill?'

'Sorry Wally,' said Alfie. 'Skint.'

'On me,' said Wally, rising from the table, his eyes scanning the rapidly filling room.

Alfie frowned as his acquaintance rose from his seat and made his way to the bar.

Times certainly had been hard since the end of what was supposed to be the war to end all wars. What with the flu outbreak and all those young men killed you'd have thought it would have been easy for the survivors to find work. Actually work was easy to find; it was getting paid for it that was difficult. That was

26

Alfie's experience, anyway. There were rumours that Willmott really wasn't as rich as she once was, but they always said that didn't they, in case they had to part with any of it.

'Ta,' he muttered as Wally thumped a fresh pint in front of him.

'You end up working all day long and go home when it's dark, too knackered to enjoy anything. In fact I'm surprised the missus is – '

'Yeah, OK,' interrupted Alfie. 'No need to keep reminding me.'

Wally surveyed the pub again, then looked back at Alfie's creased brow.

'So you're hard up?' he said eventually, wiping froth from his lips.

Alfie looked up, massaging his temples. He didn't trust Wally Barnes; never had, and their time in the army had proved him right. He was a small thin-faced man with long lank hair hanging untidily down to his shoulders and slit eyes that never seemed to look straight at you. The little finger on his right hand stuck out at a funny angle. He hated people looking at it, but the more Alfie tried not to the more he was drawn to it. A war wound, he told people, but Wally never went near the front, something of which he knew Alfie was all too well aware. He'd had it when he was born.

'I wonder what happened to the lads,' said Alfie.

'The lads?'

'At the front. Bert. Sarge. Martinsyde.'

'Dunno about Bert or Ernie Miller. Martinsyde got court-martialled though.'

'What? But he was a bloody hero. Saved us anyway.' He thought for a moment. 'Well not you, but me and Bert.'

He took a momentary pleasure at the scowl that crossed Wally's face.

'Disobeyed orders. The major wanted that chateau before the cease fire, apparently. Rumour was that there was something very pricey in there. Art or something. The major wanted it.'

'Can't see that,' said Alfie. 'Whatever it was it would have been full of bloody holes and shrapnel. More likely wanted a last bit of glory at our expense, as usual. So what happened to Martinsyde after that?'

'Dunno. You're hard up then?'

'I already said.'

Wally waited for a moment while a new customer came in and settled himself down out of earshot.

'I got a plan.'

'No Wally, I can't.'

'You haven't heard what I've got to say.'

'I can guess. Last time you had a little plan you got caught and Willmott nearly shot you.'

'Yeah, well she had that bloke with her, the one that disappeared. What happened to him anyway?'

'Dunno. No one knows. Probably couldn't get any money out of her so moved on.'

'Right, well I've got a contact who knows plants. He'll take what we can give him, the rarer the better, and give us a good price. All I need to know is where they are and which ones are worth nicking.'

'No.'

Wally sat back and looked at Alfie.

'After what little she's done for you, you still won't help an old mate nick a few plants when she's got bloody thousands of them?'

'That's right. And it's not just her, it's Jacob.'

'You think a lot of him, don't you?'

'Yes.'

'OK then. I'll do it myself. Mind you, if anyone comes along I'll have to defend myself. Probably won't be your friend Jacob.'

Alfie gasped.

'You wouldn't 'ave a go at Jacob? He wouldn't harm a fly. He's a real good 'un.'

'Well, 'corse I wouldn't actually want to, but if he was to come along and me not knowing my way around proper like, well it could happen.'

'You bastard.'

'Possibly, don't really know.'

'Well,' Alfie said, biting his lip, 'I might be able to let you know when she's away, then it would be safer. She's got places in

France and Italy and goes there a lot. Goes to London too and sometimes stays there. Maurer and Robinson are both around though; you'd have to be careful. Late at night's best.'

'I know that, don't I? When she's away they aren't going to be working late are they? They'll all be off home early if they've got any sense. And Robinson's a bloody butler, he's not going to be wandering round the gardens at night, is he? Anyway, I'd just as rather she was there. I've got a score to settle with that lady.'

'What do you mean? I thought you said you just wanted the plants, no fuss, no trouble.'

'Yeah, that's right, but like I said, I don't know my way around. Mind you, if you was to come with me then no one need get hurt.'

'I could lose my job.'

'No one will know.'

'I dunno. What's in it for me?'

Wally relaxed.

'Three ways; you, me and my buyer.'

'So I get a third. Of what?'

'You get a third of the take. After expenses.'

Alfie laughed. It was rather forced. 'Expenses?' He didn't wait for an answer. 'And what happens if the old girl comes back when we're not expecting it? Sometimes she comes back from London on the train and walks from the station late at night.'

'Now that would be a bonus,' said Wally. 'She don't make Wally Barnes look an idiot and get away with it.'

He opened his jacket just enough to let Alfie see the handle of an evil-looking knife.

'No. Any violence and I'm not interested.'

'I was only joking,' said Wally. 'Can't you see when someone's havin' a laugh? You'll just have to make sure she isn't coming back.'

Alfie looked at him. God, what was he doing getting involved with someone like this? But if he didn't help, then Jacob or Ellen Willmott could get badly hurt, or killed even. Anyway, it was true, wasn't it? She did have bags of money and didn't want to part with it. She hadn't paid him for last week yet and he'd worked hard for it. There were the kids to feed. No more credit from the local shops, that was for sure. He felt a little nauseous.

29

'Right,' he said eventually. 'But no knives.'
Wally grinned.
'No knives,' he said.

4

When that man started following us and you went to speak to him I was really worried. I'd had men follow me before, but not when I was with anyone else. Not that I knew anyone else, not properly. And not in the way that I hoped I was getting to know you.

'Excuse me for a moment,' Ken said, still looking towards the stranger.

'He's not worrying me,' Elsie said quickly. 'Can't we just ignore him?'

'Won't take a minute,' he said over his shoulder, walking towards the man who had looked up from his inspection.

Elsie looked at the fallen tree and at the roots on one side that had managed to retain some sort of grip on the ground, just enough of them to keep the tree alive even in its horizontal state. It would have been so easy for it to give up, she thought. If it was in her garden she'd be watering it, feeding it, talking to it and willing it to survive. Perhaps that's what someone did here.

'Dunno why yer wanna go wastin' yer money goin' ponsin' about with flowers,' her father had said, moving his head slightly but keeping his eyes on the television the previous night when she had told her mother where she was going.

'I'd like to go there sometime too Harry,' her mother had replied, her eyes looking wistfully into the distance.

'No you don't girl, you've got more than enough to do here.'

Elsie glanced at the bruise, nearly gone now, on her mother's face. They'd appeared after she took her mother out to the pictures one evening and they'd stopped for some chips on the way back. He'd got back from the pub before they returned and was waiting for his supper.

She remembered the anxious look on her mother's face as they approached the little two-up two-down house. The tiny front garden was neatly kept, Elsie's work, contrasting with the old wooden gate hanging crazily on one hinge. It was difficult to know whether it was the gate or the rotten post that was supporting the two of them. The paint was peeling off the old iron window frames, water dripping from a leak in the gutter forming a dirty puddle next to the front door and a loose slate hanging dangerously over their heads as Elsie inserted her key in the lock.

'Where've you soddin' been,' he'd demanded, thrusting his red sweating face at them both as they walked through the door.

'To the pictures,' said Elsie as calmly as she could manage, before turning to go upstairs to bed.

'Where do you think you're going?'

'To bed. I have work early tomorrow.' A slight stress on the 'I'.

'Don't you be like that to me young lady, this is my house and don't you forget it.'

She turned on the stairs.

'Would you like me to leave then? Of course that would be the end of my housekeeping money.'

Why couldn't she just keep her mouth shut? When he'd had too much to drink, which was most nights, he wouldn't listen to reason and was as likely as not to lash out at her mother. He did it to her once but she threatened him with the police and leaving home. He knew only too well that it was her money that kept him in beer and who knows what else, but he also suspected that she had nowhere else to go. She looked at his red face, the bulging eyes, the stomach hanging over his belt. Perhaps he wouldn't last too long now, she thought, at once feeling guilty.

She continued up to the bathroom for a quick wash, then back in her own room stripped for bed. Gazing at herself in the mirror perched on top of a battered old chest of drawers, she shuddered at the sight of her skinny body. That's when she heard the thump and the choked-off cry.

She turned and took a step towards the door, then stopped. Her mother had made her promise never to interfere. It would make things worse, she'd said. Torn with indecision, she froze, then throwing herself on to her lumpy bed, she'd pulled the bedclothes over her head and cried herself to sleep.

That was a week ago. She didn't want her mother to go through it again, not because of her obstinacy.

'Maybe one day,' she said, 'Dad might feel like a walk round there too.'

'No bloody fear,' he said. But she could tell he was mollified by being included.

She'd taken a lot of care that next morning, getting herself ready. Her father didn't get up until much later so she could take her time in the bathroom and have a leisurely breakfast. Not that she ate much, just a slice of toast and some cornflakes.

Her mother looked up from the pan of sizzling sausages as Elsie put her jacket on to leave.

'Oh you do look lovely,' she said. 'Enjoy it.' Then, laughing, 'You'll be fighting the boys off today, I know it!'

Then the laughter faded as she walked to the front door with her daughter.

'Find yourself a good man,' she whispered. 'Someone to take you away from this.'

'Mum, I couldn't leave you.'

'Elsie love, you can and you must, some day. Make it sooner rather than later.'

'No one would have me anyway,' said Elsie. 'No one I'd want to be with.'

'Are you all right?'

'Pardon?'

'You were well away, I wondered...'

'Oh, sorry Ken.' There, she'd said his name. 'I was just thinking. Did you find out what he wanted?'

'Yes, I think it's sorted.'

But the frown on his face said it wasn't.

They walked on.

Suddenly the tree-lined lane opened up and she squeezed her eyes half shut in the sudden sunlight.

'Oh dear My Lady,' he said in a mock servile accent, 'Your house has fallen down.'

'I forgot,' she said. 'I'm Ellen Willmott, aren't I!'

'Tut tut! Ellen Willmott wouldn't have forgotten she was Ellen Willmott!' he said. 'In fact no one else was allowed to forget, either.'

She laughed.

'But where's the house?'

'Come this way,' he said, taking her hand. Then, 'Oops, sorry Madam, I'm forgetting my position.'

She gripped his hand so that he couldn't let go, trying to think of a clever response but frightened of blurting out something silly.

The path seemed to go round in a big circle in front of a huge hole in the ground, guarded by a fence.

'This is the turning circle for coaches,' he explained. 'This is where I would have dropped you off if you hadn't insisted on walking. And this...'

They walked round a quarter of the circle.

'... this would have been the front of the house. Here, see the drawing. That big hole in front of us was the cellar and we are now standing at the front door. And that ruin over there – ' he pointed to a large windowless roofless building on the far side of the cellar ' – is, or rather was, your conservatory.'

They stood gazing at it for a minute or two.

'It's lovely now, but it must have been wonderful in Ellen Willmott's time,' she said. 'Were there any photographs?'

'Yes, in the information centre over there. But they are only black and white.'

He thought for a moment.

'Someone told me that a chap called Alfred Parsons spent some time painting the flowers,' he said seriously. 'But I could never understand why. They were colourful enough already. I wonder what colour he painted them.'

Her brow creased for a moment before she started to giggle, then couldn't stop.

'It wasn't that funny,' he complained.

'It was, but it's not that,' she managed to gasp. 'It's just that, well, I'm so pleased I came. I feel really happy.'

'I'm glad,' he said, giving her hand a squeeze and pretending not to notice the tears in her eyes.

'See that small building over there by the conservatory, the one with the roof on? That used to be the toilet. Now it's a sort of display area. We use it for tea break and lunch on Mondays, too.'

'We?'

'Essex Wildlife Trust volunteers. We come here each Monday to keep the place tidy, clear the leaves, renovate the walls, that sort of thing. Mostly retired people of course, being a weekday, but a few people like me work weekends and can take Mondays off.'

'You come here on your day off?'

'Yes. It's so relaxing, and the people that come have some fascinating stories to tell. Doing something useful is good, too.'

She started to ask what it was that he did do during the rest of the week, but stopped herself just in time.

'Right my lady,' he said, guiding her back to the main path. 'We shall see how your orchard garden has survived.'

The path dived back into the trees, but they soon left it to turn into a much narrower path.

'Kenneth!' she said. 'You really have let this go, haven't you.'

He grinned. 'Yes madam. But look, you can still make out the old rockery there. OK, so there are only snowdrops there now, but you can imagine what it was like, can't you?'

'Oh yes, Ken,' she murmured. 'I really can.'

The old sycamore stump sticking up in the middle, the leaf mould in the sunken walkway, the grass growing amongst the rocks, none of that mattered. She could see Ellen Willmott walking round, bending to pick a weed out or to examine a flower more closely, or to breathe in the fragrance.

'And that's a *Meliosma* tree,' said Ken, pointing to a tree that looked rather as if it was about to expire.

'A what?'

'A *Meliosma* tree.'

'Right. What does it do? It's an orchard area, so presumably it produces fruit? Where is it from?'

'Er,' said Ken looking rather discomfited. 'Actually I haven't asked anyone. I know it's rare so people are supposed to be impressed, but I don't know much about it.'

Elsie smiled, deciding not to mention the slightly pink hue Ken's face had taken on.

'But I do know that although it used to be an orchard area Ellen Willmott turned it into a flower garden. She kept some ornamental or rare trees, but the rest had to go. Food was grown over the road. Flowers were her first love.' He pointed to a drift of white flowers thirty or forty centimetres high on the other side of the path. ' I don't know if she planted those though.'

'Should I know what they are?'

'No, probably not,' he grinned. 'I'm only pointing them out to get you off the *Meliosma* tree. They are three-cornered leek.'

Elsie bent and examined one.

'Bl.. er.. blooms are nice.'

Ken burst out laughing. 'You are allowed to say "Bloody hell, they stink" if you like.'

'They do rather, don't they,' she said, blushing. 'But I can't see any corners'

'Just feel the stems.'

'Oh yes, they've got corners on them. Three.'

'Come on, give me your book,' he said, 'I'll write the Latin name. It's *Allium triquetrum*. Actually I can't remember whether it's garlic or leek. Leek, I think.'

Elsie bent down again while he was writing. 'What's that?' she asked, pointing to a small oval disc just about showing in among the flowers.

'Good gracious, you've got sharp eyes,' said Ken admiringly. 'I thought all those had been found. It's one of Ellen Willmott's plant labels.'

He bent down, pulled it out and passed it to her. The label itself was in remarkably good condition, although the stalk that it had been soldered on to had mostly rusted away. She rubbed the dirt off.

'It's got an S, with a WT beneath it and an eight beneath that,' she said. 'What does it mean?'

'I've no idea,' admitted Ken. 'I think it's Ellen Willmott's code for one of her hybrids, but I'm not sure. I'll let Robin or David have it and they can add it to their collection.'

'Before you do, can I draw it?'

'Of course. I'll have to get you a camera,' Ken said, grinning.

'I prefer drawing, I think,' said Elsie, sticking the label back into the ground and pulling out her sketchbook. 'One of her special plants,' she murmured as she quickly drew the label and its code, before sketching the flowers in which she found it. Then, pulling it from the ground once more, she stroked it before handing it to Ken.

'Ellen Willmott must have held that,' she said.

'Almost certainly,' agreed Ken. 'Later I'll show you what we've collected if you like.'

'That would be nice.'

She glowed with pleasure inside. She had found something the rest of them had missed, and it was something Ellen Willmott had placed there, she was sure of that.

They walked on, past the tree of heaven and innumerable holly bushes, round the remains of the cold frames, stopped briefly at some rather deep concrete-lined reservoirs, until finally they approached a high wall, over which she could see the tops of magnolias and also some trees she couldn't recognise. The path led to an opening and as they walked through she froze.

'It's beautiful,' she gasped. 'I've never seen anything like it.'

'It is pretty, isn't it,' agreed Ken.

The ground was covered in white snowdrops, purple crocuses, anemones, scillas, and others she could not put a name to. The magnolia trees were in pink bloom, and a camellia was in flower too. Surrounding them all was a wall the like of which she had never seen before, fully three metres tall she thought, with plants climbing the pitted bricks whichever way she looked.

'Oh Ken,' she said, tearing her eyes away from the colour and looking at him, 'it's wonderful.'

As he smiled back at her, they heard a polite cough from someone trying to get through.

'Oh hello Ken,' said a smiling woman leading a small group of visitors, her eye flicking briefly to their joined hands.

'Hello Daphne,' said Ken a little self-consciously. 'I'm just showing Elsie round.'

'Hello Elsie, I'm Daphne. It's so lovely in the spring, isn't it?'

'Oh yes,' agreed Elsie, feeling immediately at ease. 'It's my first time.'

'I hope you can come again then.'

She smiled at Ken and led her group into the garden.

They let the group go on ahead.

'She thinks you're my boyfriend,' whispered Elsie.

'I would like to be,' said Ken. 'That is, unless you've already got – '

'No,' she said quickly. 'I haven't. I'd love to see you again, but you don't know me. Where I come from, what I do, anything really.'

'I know enough about you Elsie. The rest doesn't matter.'

Oh yes it does, she thought.

'That's a *Ginkgo biloba* tree,' he said pointing to an enormous tree in one corner of the garden. 'The leaves are very distinctive and they go a lovely yellow in the autumn.'

'Would Ellen Willmott have planted that?' she asked.

'I don't know. It looks older than that to me, but I'm not an expert. If we see Frank I'll ask him.'

'Frank?'

'He's the warden. He knows a lot about this place and trees in general.'

'That one, for instance,' he continued, pointing to a much smaller but nevertheless old-looking tree with huge leaves, 'was commonly thought to be an Umbrella tree, *Magnolia tripetala*. He said it was a Japanese large-leafed magnolia, *Magnolia obovata*, and when other experts looked at it they found he was more likely to be right.'

'But if it's a magnolia why isn't it flowering like the others?'

'Very observant. It actually flowers much later than them. Much later than most magnolias in fact.'

She stood absentmindedly brushing her hand across the top of the low box hedging and taking in the myriad of scents from all about her. Everything was so beautiful, she thought.

They started to walk again and her heart sank for a moment as he let go of her hand. Then she felt it closing round her waist and she reached round his body and squeezed. It couldn't last, they were from different worlds, but she'd enjoy it while it did.

'Right,' he said as they finally left the walled garden. 'This is Ellen Willmott's conservatory. She sat in it to relax, write letters, that sort of thing.' He pointed to a path along the outside of the wall 'That way is the daffodil bank, a boating lake that no longer has any water in it, and some excellent trees. But we won't go there today.'

'Oh, why not?' she asked, frowning slightly.

'Because I want to make sure you come back to complete the walk,' he chuckled. 'Although if you like we can have a look at the North Pond from a bird hide.'

'Oh yes, I've never seen a bird hide.'

'Really? They usually just fly up into the tree and get behind some leaves.'

'Pardon?'

'Birds. That's how they hide.'

'Oh Ken!' she spluttered, trying not to look silly having a fit of the giggles.

'Sorry, it not my fault it's who I work with here,' he grinned. 'It's just an old shed with slits for windows facing the pond. It might be boring, but we could be lucky and see some birds coming to feed.'

They walked along the outside of the wall, stopping to look at the flowers filling the bed at its foot, before descending the slope towards the hide.

They soon came to a small shed and Ken quietly eased the door open. Elsie was pleased to see that it wasn't occupied and they went in. It was pitch black in there and she had a sudden feeling that he might take her in his arms and kiss her, but to her disappointment he opened the shutter over the window and light flooded in.

They sat on the little bench and looked out.

The pond, surrounded by trees, wasn't a large one but was big enough to contain several islands, each at least as big as her garden at home.

'One of our jobs,' he whispered, 'is to pull up the Himalayan balsam and pile them up on those islands. They decompose and go back into the soil.'

'Are there any fish in the pond?'

'None of us have ever seen any, and we've paddled in it often enough clearing it out.'

She felt a thrill as his arm slid round her waist. Strange how different it was from anything she had experienced in the past. She put her own round him, hoping he would kiss her.

Eventually, to her disappointment, he gave her a final squeeze and got to his feet.

'Come on, we'd best be getting back.'

He helped her up the steep steps until they were back at the walled garden and they strolled slowly down towards the turning circle. Why couldn't it have gone on longer?

'I forgot to tell you,' he said as they reached the main drive. 'That's the walnut tree. It's very old. You can see how some of the branches are tied together to stop them breaking off, and the trunk has been buttressed with concrete. Ellen Willmott did that when the trunk went hollow on one side and the tree was in danger of falling over. Are you all right?'

'Yes, I'm fine,' she said.

'But you're shivering.'

'Honestly, I really am fine. It's just that a strange feeling came over me.'

He held her tight.

'Come on then, let's go back.'

'Do we have to? I don't want it to stop.'

'It doesn't have to,' he said. 'We'll go to the *Thatchers* and have a drink and perhaps a sandwich. Then I'll take you home.'

She froze.

'Or at least drop you off in Brentwood,' he said.

'That would be nice, thank-you.'

She sensed his disappointment and knew he was wondering where he stood as he turned and they started to walk back down the drive to the exit. Oh God, it was all going wrong. She stopped and turned to face him, tilted her face up and put her arms round him. He bent down and she shut her eyes as his lips met hers. She wanted the kiss to last for ever, but eventually opened her eyes to draw breath and saw, over his shoulder, the blonde man standing by the path beneath a tree, watching them.

5

I loved the way you told me about Ellen Willmott and Jacob
Maurer. You really brought them to life. I'd have liked Jacob.
He'd have told me about the flowers. I think I'd have been a bit
frightened of Ellen Willmott though.

Jacob Maurer knew better than to interrupt Ellen Willmott as they
stood looking out across the ha-ha at the walnut tree. Although
several years had passed since the Kaiser's defeat, her fortunes
had not improved with the coming of peace. But Jacob was well
aware that the war was far from her thoughts; when she lapsed
into sad reflections such as this it was Alex who was on her mind.
She admitted as much on one occasion when her thoughts became
too much to bear alone and broke through her iron facade, but
was irritable for the rest of the day, Jacob remembered.

Poor Alex. They both referred to him by that name, rather than
his real name, Charles, which they had discovered later. It was
hard to imagine the torment he must have suffered. Jacob had
known then that Ellen Willmott would never really get over it,
and she never had. He had briefly been the son she had always
wanted.

'The walnut tree,' she said at last. 'If we do not concrete it
now it will be too late.'

The tree had been deteriorating for years and she had decided
that as a last resort the side of the trunk, now hollow and open to
the elements, should be filled with concrete to stabilise it. Alex
had prepared the shuttering round the base of the tree shortly
before he died, but had not had time to pour the concrete. It had
stood like that ever since.

Jacob looked round.

'Alfie,' he called. 'Come here please.'

The tall well-built figure wearing a cloth cap and the
regulation apron that all the gardeners wore put his rake aside and
came from further down the carriageway.

'It's getting late now, but tomorrow morning get started on
concreting the tree,' he said. 'Check the shuttering first, but I

think it's still serviceable. It must be finished before Miss Willmott gets back.'

'Yes sir,' said Alfie, shuffling his feet.

'Is there a problem?'

'Well, er, I haven't been paid for last week Mr Maurer. And if Madam is going away...'

Ellen Willmott stared at the walnut tree.

'Have you ever not been paid, though perhaps a few days after the normal time?' asked Jacob.

'Well, no, but the butcher does like his money before he cuts our meat.'

'And no doubt the barman likes the same before he draws the ale,' said Jacob dryly. 'You may take a rabbit if you can get one, and some potatoes from my garden. I am sure Robinson will provide your wages shortly.'

The gardener drew a breath as if to reply, looked at Ellen Willmott and with a muttered 'Thank-you' shuffled off to return to his rake while she stared at his back.

'He really does not mean any insubordination,' commented Jacob. 'He's a good lad. But times are hard for them, especially those with families. Coming back from the war has been difficult. They all expected – well, hoped for – so much.'

'He has a good knowledge of the garden as a whole?'

'Oh yes. The Alpine garden is his favourite place, but he is interested in everything he comes across.'

'The Field Club; could he manage them?'

'Yes. It would be good experience for him, too.'

'Do not mention it. I may change my mind. The boating lake I think.'

Jacob smiled to himself. She could be hard at times but occasionally, despite her best efforts, a soft streak appeared. The Essex Field Club usually came up with a whip-round after their tour if they were impressed with their guide and it would be a real boost for Alfie. Jacob would make sure it went well but could not risk telling him of his mistress's suggestion; it was quite possible that she would indeed change her mind.

Alfie Hedges now far from her thoughts, Ellen Willmott turned to go up the path at the side of the house.

Briefly stopping to examine the *Umbellularia californica*, the headache tree, she turned at the rear of the building round the corner of the conservatory. Stopping once again her gaze went along the outside of the south wall of the walled garden. The border here was filled with spring bulbs, such as a variety of wood anemones and she could just see the *Campanula lactiflora* pushing through and – oh dear, was that the violet flowers of ground ivy? Then, slower now, she walked the few yards further, pausing at the garden house, and into the walled garden itself.

As they entered she looked at the *Ginkgo biloba* tree, the flourishing Chusan palm, the box hedging, the spindle tree – but her eyes kept flicking back to the south wall where Jacob had first started Alex doing repair work.

'I miss him,' said Jacob softly.

Ellen Willmott nodded, pulled herself together, and moved on and out of the far side, stopping to look past the hothouse to the beech tree standing on the outside of the far corner of the garden.

'That will come down one day when the wind is strong,' she said. 'And when it does it will make short work of the hothouse; and possibly the wall, but hopefully not while I am here.'

Jacob sighed at the sight of the sycamores growing all around. He just couldn't keep up with them, not with the staff at his disposal. At least, for once, Ellen Willmott refrained from commenting on them.

Walking further on alongside the north field, they stopped by the Caucasian wing-nut tree. Jacob saw that his mistress was smiling.

'I was walking once along here with Alex,' she explained. 'We saw a thief trying to steal my flowers. He produced a rather long knife when Alex tried to apprehend him, and wanted my bag. He got a bit of a shock instead – my bullet hit the tree inches from his head. He ran for his life.'

'Lucky you weren't aiming to hit him, then,' said Jacob.

'No, he was most fortunate,' she said. 'But I wonder sometimes if he will come back. The bullet would have been only a temporary bar to his greed and I am surprised the awful man hasn't paid us another visit.'

They walked on slowly.

'The lake has trouble holding its water,' she commented.

'Roots have penetrated the clay,' suggested Jacob. 'I'll get it seen to.'

'If you find the time,' she replied, 'but there are more pressing needs and I have little time for boating lately, nor visiting this far from the house.'

Passing round the end of the boating lake they started on the steep climb up to Evelyn's chestnuts. Jacob tactfully stopped to look across the meadow.

'The daffodils were superb this year,' he commented.

She smiled. That was what made Jacob so special.

They reached the top and stopped again to look at the Spanish chestnuts and beyond at the smoky city of London.

She turned and looked briefly at the summerhouse where she had found the final secret of Alex's identity, before walking purposefully on.

Jacob too quickened his pace, pleased to be nearing his beloved alpine garden. They crossed the bridge over the gorge, stopping for a moment at the edge to look at the array of alpine plants tumbling down amongst the rocks to the stream below.

'I don't know how you do it,' she said to Jacob. 'It still looks beautiful.'

'It's my life,' he said.

Leaving her gardener she walked on down the slope to the drive, returning to the big house.

Jacob found himself in the same reflective mood as his employer as he eased himself down on to a rock and looked at the gorge, the south pond and his cottage beyond. This was indeed his whole life. His cousin Friedi was very good, looking after the children as she did; a little stern at times perhaps, but maybe that was what was needed. He missed Rosina though, missed her terribly, as did the children. How cruel fate was to take her away like that after all that she had been through. Should he have brought her here from her native Switzerland? Would she still be alive if he had not? No one could answer that question and there was no point in dwelling upon it, but it was hard not to do so.

What a pity his employer didn't settle down with someone, he thought. The doctor perhaps; he was a good man, her equal, and they seemed to get on very well. It might take the rough edges off her, he conjectured. Much though Jacob respected her, not only for her position but also for her various talents, her tongue was something to be feared. Although they shared a passion for the garden, their way of dealing with people could not have been more different. She ruled not only by her superior knowledge, but by fear; his knowledge was equal to hers but his men gave their best because of their respect, even love, for him. He thought his way was the best and it was indeed the only way he could manage his staff; she no doubt thought he was too soft, but recognised the results even if she could not understand how he achieved them.

He rose to his feet and clambered down to the main drive, then along the path to his cottage. Taking out his knife he cut some flowers from his garden and tied them with twine.

'I won't be long,' he called out to Friedi.

She knew where he was going and would keep his dinner until his return.

He trudged along the outside of the big wall towards Brentwood, his thoughts now far from the garden behind it, no longer feeling his aching limbs. Past the Headley Arms, past Warley Barracks, past Warley Hospital, until he came to a little side-road on his left, Cemetery Road, only a hundred yards or so long with an iron fence and large gate across the far end, and a smaller one beside it. He made his way through, down the path past the little chapel and the neat rows of gravestones, and came to a stop at a small yew tree. He wished he could have afforded a proper headstone but the tree was already bigger and prettier than any block of marble. There he laid his flowers.

6

They really took the Mickey out of me when I told them about you. They are very good at worming all the details out of anyone they think is hiding anything. I didn't tell them everything though. Not how I felt about you. I couldn't put that into words.

Elsie got to the office early that evening. Some of the staff were still working, so although she wanted to sing she kept quiet. She put her overall on, made sure her hair was tied up, got the big plastic sack and started going along between the two rows of desks emptying the waste bins. They were a decent lot here actually. Always had a good word to say. Well most of them, anyway.

'Good weekend Elsie?'

'Very, thanks. You?'

'Yes, me too.'

She wanted to tell them about Warley Place, but they were staying late to catch up with their work, not to listen to her. Well she supposed that was why they stayed. On the other hand they might just want the extra money. If they got any, that is. She wondered if Ken worked in an office. She'd ask him next time – if there was a next time. He'd said to go again, but people said that sort of thing, didn't they? It didn't necessarily follow that they meant it. He'd kissed her though. Not in the selfish almost lewd way that some of the locals had kissed her in the past, but in a gentle, caring, but still very sensual way. She'd sat down and shut her eyes when she got back home and imagined that kiss, again and again. Her mum had smiled at her when she opened her eyes. She hadn't said anything, but she knew.

It had been difficult asking him to stop in the town rather than outside her house. She'd almost relented, but was scared. It was all very well in stories, the man not worrying about such things, but she wasn't so sure about real life. Perhaps next time.

His hands didn't feel like an office worker's hands. Not that she really knew what an office worker's hands felt like. His were cared for, but used to the outside. Not rough though. Perhaps he worked in an office but played football or cricket.

'Bye Elsie.'

'Bye.'

That was the last of them, on his way home. You could tell a lot about her men from the contents of their bins. Gerry's didn't have a lot in it and the paper was often used on both sides. There was actually a big yellow bag they were supposed to use for waste paper and they did when there was a lot of it, but odd sheets they just dropped in their bins. She didn't mind, she just pulled them out and put them in the yellow sack. If he ate in the office he took his apple cores home. Freddy's had all sorts of rubbish in it – crisp packets, Mars wrappers, newspapers, orange peel and once an old pair of trainers. She'd taken them out just in case it was a mistake but they were there again the next day.

Dragging her sack to the stairwell, she got the spray polish and cloth out. They had a clear desk policy here as far as their work was concerned, which made her job much easier. The staff were told to get all their papers off their desks before they went home. She'd thought it was to help the cleaners until one of them said it was partly for security and partly in case there was a fire. She left the computer screens where they were, but lifted the mouse and mouse mat with one hand, gave the desk a quick squirt and rub, put the mouse back and it was done.

She picked up the framed picture on Gerry Bailey's desk; a close-up of him and his wife, standing looking at each other, smiling. She wondered if Ken would ever have a picture like that on his desk; him and her together.

She was glad he didn't know about her job. Not that there was anything wrong with what she did, but well, it didn't require much in the way of an intellect, did it? She felt ashamed at the thought; ashamed for thinking that about her mates. And a bit ashamed that she thought Ken might mind.

She finished the desk tops and pulled the yellow bag for the waste paper along to the stairwell alongside the rubbish bag. Then, opening her cupboard, she got the vacuum cleaner out and wheeled it back into the office. Plugging the retractable lead in she went to push the 'on' switch with her foot.

'Tea up,' she heard.

Oh God. Now for the interrogation. They all had tea on the third floor and caught up with the gossip, especially after the weekend. What was that name again? Tithatch? No. Nuthatch, that was it. She'd tell them about that. And the snowdrops. Gal... galan... No, give that a miss. They'd definitely laugh if she tried to pronounce it. She'd tried to when she told her mother about it all, but had to look in her book and her father had mocked her attempts and told her she was stupid. She'd ignored him at first, but the happier she got when she was talking to her mother the more annoyed he became. It was as if he didn't want her to do anything to improve herself. Actually he didn't, she knew that already. What she couldn't work out was why.

Kelly had made the tea. They took it in turns, one each day. With five of them it worked out well, Elsie's day being Friday. She picked up her mug, the one with flowers on it.

'Saw a smashing film on Saturday,' said Kelly. 'With Freddie.'

'You still with him?' That was Mary. 'I thought he was history?'

'He was. Now he's back again. With a new car.'

'Back to his place after then? Come on, out with it.'

'Bet that's what Kelly said when they got there!' giggled Ruby.

They all burst into hysterical laughter.

'What about you then Ruby?' They knew the details of Kelly's affairs already and also knew that most of them were figments of her imagination.

'Oh, me and Jake stayed in and watched telly. Well I watched telly. He was more interested in getting a view down my front.'

'I went to Warley Place,' volunteered Elsie.

'Oh yes, I remember you said you was,' said Kelly. 'What about you Mary? Do anything interesting?'

'I met someone,' said Elsie, flushing a little at the rebuff.

'Oh smashing,' said Pam. She was the quiet one of the group, quieter even than Elsie and sensitive of hurt when she saw it. 'What was he like?'

'Really handsome. Dark hair, a couple of years older than me. Knows an awful lot about plants and things. He's in the Essex Wildlife Trust.'

'Come on Else, we don't want to know all that,' said Ruby. 'What was he like in bed?'

'We didn't go to bed. He's a gentleman.'

'Boring!' said Kelly.

'He wants to see me again though.'

'That's good,' said Pam. 'You could do with someone like that.'

'We saw a bird that walks up and down trees.'

'Woodpecker,' announced Mary.

'What's it walk for when it's got wings?' giggled Kelly. 'Must be a stupid bird.'

'Woodpeckers only walk up trees,' said Elsie. 'Not down. It's a nuthatch. They are the only ones to walk down. And they do it while they are looking for insects in the bark, that's why they don't – '

'Freddie's taking me to Southend in his car tonight,' broke in Kelly.

Elsie slowly got up from her seat and washed her mug.

'Must get on,' she said, her face red.

'You are an ignorant lot,' she heard Pam say as she started climbing the stairs. But she knew she was kidding herself if she thought there was any future with Ken. As soon as he saw where she lived, as soon as he found out what she did, as soon as he knew how little she knew about life, he'd be off. Oh, he'd be very gentlemanly about it, but he'd go nevertheless. Why couldn't she be satisfied with someone whose ambitions started and ended with groping inside her blouse? Why not stay with her own kind?

Jamie had been after her for ages. His dad was one of her father's friends. Her father reckoned she could do worse. So she could, but not much. She reached her floor and stood looking at the empty desks.

'You all right Elsie?' It was Pam, coming up behind her. 'They don't mean nothing. A bit jealous, that's all.'

'I know. He was lovely though.'

'Be careful Elsie. If he's like you say, you could get hurt. Best to stay with our own kind, that way you know where you are.'

'But he's different,' Elsie said helplessly.

'Yes, probably,' said Pam unconvincingly. 'Well, must go. I hope it works for you.'

'Thanks,' said Elsie lifting the nozzle of the vacuum cleaner and pushing the switch with her foot, her mouth tight and a little tear starting at the corner of one of her eyes.

She moved all the chairs and the now empty bins to the middle of the office so that she could vacuum under the desks. Some of the cleaners didn't bother, just doing round them, but Elsie liked to do the job properly even if it did take a bit longer.

By the time she had pushed the chairs and bins back into place and cleaned the central corridor her irritation with her friends had faded. She stood there for a moment, having a last look at her office. She took a pride in leaving it spotless. Sometimes she found she'd left a bin in the wrong place, or a desk not properly tidied, but not today. Today everything was sparkling and in its place. There was nothing wrong with the job or her mates, she told herself. But she did want something better out of life. She'd join the Essex Wildlife Trust, that's what she'd do. She'd gradually learn more about flowers, and perhaps trees as well. She'd like to join them on their Monday work, but it was awkward. She did cleaning for houses, mostly old people, during the day, her office cleaning was in the evening, so she could fit it in with a bit of juggling, but he'd ask how she managed to get the time off. Well she would tell him. Yes, that's what she would do. She'd tell him what she did. If he didn't like it, well, that was an end to it. But she'd join the Wildlife Trust anyway. Probably.

7

I wonder how Ellen Willmott's sister Rose felt when she became part of the Berkeley family. Did she feel like I felt at Warley Place, a bit over-awed by it all? If she was anything like her sister I expect she took it all in her stride.

'I shall be all right,' said Ellen Willmott to Robinson. 'Stop fussing. I am going to Spetchley and that's that.'

'But who will go with you?' asked Robinson, his brow furrowed with concern.

Ellen Willmott's lady's maid of many years, Eliza Burge, who often accompanied her on these trips when Robinson was otherwise engaged, had died during the war and had not been replaced. Well, one had to make sacrifices when times were hard, she told herself. Anyway, no one could adequately replace Eliza.

Robinson had proved a good travelling companion for her in the past, but he was too busy filling in for the gaps in the staff at the moment and keeping an eye on the few that were left. They were even missing a housekeeper right at the moment, after she had to dismiss the last one. The wretched woman had the nerve to say she was going to leave anyway. She was definitely getting above herself, that one, and probably stealing things if the truth were known. Anyway, Robinson really couldn't be spared.

'I am perfectly well able to travel on my own,' she snapped. 'If you just accompany me to Paddington Station, that will be sufficient. Have you organised the brougham?'

'Yes Miss Willmott,' he sighed. 'It should be here at any moment.'

'Something amuses you, Robinson?'

'Simply your insistence upon your independence, Miss Willmott,' he said.

She stared at him for a moment. They got on well, she and Robinson. He was as trusted and loyal as any servant could be, but sometimes something she said or did amused him and she rarely discovered what it was. It showed in his eyes; or was it his mouth twitching almost imperceptibly?

'You weren't going to suggest that I took the autobus?' she asked eventually, her eyes narrowing.

'Good gracious, it would be most unbecoming for you to travel in that way.'

The bus service had recently been extended to Great Warley and although useful for the hoi polloi it wasn't something she ever intended to use.

She looked up at the sound of a horse's hooves and the brougham came into view.

'I shall be accompanying Miss Willmott to Paddington,' Robinson called up to the coachman as the horses came to a standstill.

He helped his mistress up into the cab and walked round to the other side to enter with her small bag. The majority of the luggage had been sent on earlier; not that she took much these days. Her eyes turned to the big house across the road as the coach left the carriageway at North Lodge and emerged onto the main thoroughfare to Brentwood.

'We all miss her,' Robinson said softly.

She nodded. Her sister Rose had lived there, at Warley Lea, for a while after her marriage to Robert Berkeley and it was indeed pleasant to have her so close before they moved to Spetchley Park in Worcestershire, her destination today. The treatment Rose was having for her cancer was proving insufficient to other than prolong her life a little and the end was not far away. For all she knew this could be the last time they would meet.

She looked ahead, giving the little cemetery in Warley just a passing glance, and in only a few minutes they were drawing to a halt outside the station. With the train running on time and Robinson's usual immaculate planning they had very little time to wait before being seated on the train to Liverpool Street.

'So what action have you taken to find a new housekeeper?' she asked.

He told her what she already knew; that the usual agents had been informed and that a reply was awaited.

She hoped he wouldn't ask too many questions about where the money was coming from to pay the gardening staff or the utility bills, or indeed his own remuneration. She knew only too well what a problem that was for him, when really it was her own responsibility, but she really couldn't face it, what with Rose being so ill. Otherwise she would certainly have sorted it out.

At least there was a view from these windows, she thought, as the train sped its way to the city. Once they got there and on to the Metropolitan underground train the noise and smell inside those tunnels was truly awful.

The factories and houses backing onto the railway became more and more numerous – how could people live so close to a railway line? – and the air itself seemed to be composed mostly of fumes as they drew closer to Liverpool Street. Finally the high pitched noise of the steel wheels on the rails lowered its tone as the train slowed and swayed over the points before lurching to a stop alongside the platform.

She allowed Robinson to assist her in alighting from the carriage, thankful that she had only the one small bag with her on this occasion. Even when she had sent her main luggage on in advance she often found at the last moment that she needed to take more than she could conveniently carry. That had not previously been a problem for her, not when Robinson or her housekeeper accompanied her, but since she started going on her own it was not really an option.

She felt her stomach tighten as they made their way down the tunnel. Not that she suffered from claustrophobia, but this really was not a pleasant place to be. Once on the underground train she just closed her eyes and did her best not to get bounced about as the train made its noisy and unsteady way to Paddington.

Her head was beginning to ache by the time they were able to transfer to the Great Western Railway train and Robinson found an empty non-smoking women's compartment. He helped her in, put her bag on the luggage rack above her head, and, leaving the carriage, closed the door.

'Thank-you Robinson,' she said through the open window as he waited for the train to leave, standing by the door to deter unsuitable women from entering. 'I fear I have not been good company this day. At least you will have some peace for a while.'

'The place is empty when you are not there Miss Willmott,' he said. 'But you can leave the house to me and the garden to Jacob with an easy mind.'

She nodded in thankful agreement as with a whistle and the slipping of wheels on the rails the train slowly began to move.

She settled back in her seat, pleased that with her butler's help she had the carriage to herself and closed her eyes. She was indeed fortunate to have such a man.

She used to find these journeys so peaceful. The one o'clock train was an express, so it was unlikely that anyone would join her in the currently otherwise empty compartment; a steely look usually resolved the problem if a passenger from elsewhere in the train did try to enter from the corridor. There was a Luncheon and Tea Car, but she had not booked a meal. The train arrived in Worcester at a quarter to four, so a sandwich prepared by her cook earlier would suffice until she reached her destination.

This was a time to relax and watch the countryside go by; a time to reflect on the good things of life and the pleasures awaiting her at Spetchley Park. The gardens there were indeed beautiful. Not as exotic as her own, she tried to persuade herself, but very grand. She felt a twinge of envy knowing that they would continue to be so for very many years to come whereas even she could see that the future for her own creation was very uncertain indeed.

She was looking forward to seeing her sister Rose again, but worried sick at how ill she was getting. Hopefully she would be up to a walk round the gardens, even if Ellen had to push her in a bath chair or they travelled in a carriage. Walking was best though, one could stop much more easily to admire this plant or that.

Her relationship with Rose had never faltered over the years, but recently she wondered about her welcome at Spetchley Park. She was always received with the utmost civility and had to admit that Rose had an excellent husband in Robert Berkeley. The Berkeley family was one of the oldest and most respected families in the land and Rose, from comparatively humble origins, had been accepted readily into their circle.

Ellen Willmott was well aware that one of the reasons Spetchley Park had survived and prospered for over three hundred years was the judicious management of the estate, enabling it to be passed down intact from one generation to the next. Her brother-in-law had urged her to cut down on her spending, many times; he had produced figures showing that she could not afford to carry on as she was, but figures could be made to show what accountants wanted them to, couldn't they? She knew in her heart that the advice she received was based on experience accumulated over many years, generations in fact, and she would do well to act on his counsel. But she had no heir, she thought stubbornly; she had no one to hand her estate down to and she wanted to enjoy her garden while she still could. Perhaps the Royal Horticultural Society would take it over when she went? After all, it was admired by royalty so what better final home for it?

After taking a brief snack, more to relieve the boredom than to satisfy any hunger, she dozed off and woke with a start as the train came shuddering to a halt at Worcester Shrub Hill Station.

The liveried figure of a footman came hurrying from further along the platform as she alighted.

'Miss Willmott?' he asked. 'I have the brougham a short distance away but can have it brought closer if – '

'If I can walk round my estate I think I can manage to walk a few yards to a carriage,' she snapped, immediately regretting the outburst but unwilling to apologise. She was relieved to be able to thank him when he helped her up into the brougham and saw his stony face relax a little.

The journey to Spetchley Park was a little longer than that from Warley Place to Brentwood and, despite the pleasing scenery, she was glad when at last the horse's hooves were crunching up the gravel on the long winding path between the trees. They soon reached the entrance to the big Georgian house. Built of Bath stone early in the nineteenth century, replacing the earlier Tudor house which was burned to the ground to prevent it being used as Cromwell's headquarters before the Battle of Worcester almost two centuries earlier, it was indeed an imposing edifice with its four big pillars and wide steps at the entrance making her own house seem small.

'Rose!' she exclaimed as her sister appeared at the top of the steps. 'How lovely to see you again.'

Her heart sank as her beloved sister smiled a welcome. She had not looked at all well when they had last met, but now she looked far worse. She mounted the stone steps quickly, ignoring the pain in her knees, in case Rose should attempt to come down to her, and took her in her arms.

'Thank goodness we live in modern times and have a railway to transport us speedily across the country without too much inconvenience,' she continued.

'Inconvenience enough I fear,' said Rose. 'You look tired.'

'Nonsense, not too tired to see how our garden progresses,' Ellen assured her.

'Do you need me madam?' enquired the footman, waiting patiently after accompanying Ellen Willmott up the steps in case she should fall.

'I don't think so Walter,' she said. 'Perhaps when Miss Willmott has rested and eaten we may take a short ride round the gardens.'

'I have been resting for the whole of the interminable journey,' exclaimed Ellen Willmott, 'and ate my fill on the railway train. I have been looking forward all day to seeing how the garden has developed. But I am happy to wait until tomorrow if you yourself would rather do so.'

'No, I too have been waiting to show you what I have done,' Rose said animatedly, but then with a frown, 'I do hope you will approve.'

'If you like it I will like it,' said her sister.

'Very well. Walter, could you take us to the walled garden where...' she paused to look at the sky, '... no, I fear we do not have sufficient time before darkness is upon us. Just take us to the bridge. You can wait by the Horse Pool and we will join you there.' She turned to her sister. 'We will postpone our tour of the whole garden until tomorrow.'

The footman helped them up into the cab of the brougham and they sat in silence as the carriage slowly made its way through the avenue of maples, ashes and oaks towards their destination. The *Crocus tommasinianus* beneath the trees were past their best but still pretty, and the Martagon lilies that would take over from them were not yet out in their full beauty.

Stopping the carriage and dismounting at the small footbridge spanning the moat and the extension to the garden pool, it was but a short walk past the conservatory to the Fountain Gardens.

Although Rose discussed the whole garden with her husband and the head gardener, she and her sister had designed what was termed the Fountain Garden. With a large fountain at the centre, it was divided into four compartments by close-clipped yew hedging. Each one of the compartments was then divided into nine further gardens, the whole therefore comprising thirty-six beds. They had developed the idea of each bed representing a different botanical family and planted it thus. Like most gardens, as it grew, ways of making it more attractive became apparent. Some they discussed during Ellen Willmott's visits, others Rose implemented herself.

'Rose, it's lovely,' said Ellen Willmott as they wound their way through the paths round the various beds. 'You have done wonders.'

They stopped for a moment to look more closely at a tree peony 'Souvenir de Maxime Cornu'.

'What a shame it hasn't flowered yet,' commented Ellen Willmott. 'It's going to be beautiful later this month. But see, 'Lord Kitchener' is in bloom. Just look at those flowers.'

The several different varieties of magnolia; the acers with their orange-red peeling bark; the sorbuses; it was indeed a spectacle and it was with some reluctance that they finally left to face the colourful south border of the Kitchen Garden.

They stopped first at *Xanthoceras sorbifolium*, a Chinese shrub that was rarely seen outside that country, its white flowers showing brightly in erect panicles. Then Ellen Willmott looked briefly at the *Ginkgo biloba* standing proudly against the wall, went as if to speak but kept her silence. Her sister pealed with laughter.

'You were going to say that your own *Ginkgo* is just a little larger, were you not?' she said.

'Oh Rose,' replied her sister, mortified. 'Am I that transparent? Am I that envious? Surely not.'

'You are proud of what you have achieved,' said Rose. 'And so you should be.'

Oh how she missed her sister, thought Ellen Willmott as they turned and made their way down the west border and its equally impressive array of plants, to the Horse Pool and the waiting carriage. She really was lonely sometimes at Warley Place.

'Now,' said Rose, sipping her drink back at the house, 'we are both weary, you especially after your long journey, but before I let you retire, tell me of Warley Place.'

'Warley Place is, well, Warley Place.'

'What of Robinson? Is he fit and well?'

'Robinson is always fit and well, mentally and physically.'

'And Jacob? How is Jacob dealing with Rosina's sad death?'

'Jacob does not share his worries with others; does not allow them to affect his work. I think perhaps that is how he deals with them. He immerses himself in his precious alpines. How I rely on him!'

'Does he still write all those letters?'

'Oh yes, every evening as I understand it. He sips his home-made wine and writes to his sisters.'

'I thought he might get together with Maggie at some stage. She seems such a sweet girl.'

'Well, yes, maybe, but to take on nine of someone else's children, that would take some doing. Well, eight now Max has gone back to Switzerland. A shame really, from what I saw of him I quite liked Max. A little too boisterous at times, but he had spirit. They are all good children; perhaps it is because he is the eldest. Anyway, Friedi keeps them in order and they are always clean and well-fed.'

'So what about you, Ellen?'

'What about me?'

'The doctor. I thought perhaps...'

'The doctor is a fine man, but wedded to his career. He would have little time for me.'

'And of course you are wedded to your garden and would have little time for him?'

'That is different. He could always retire and help with mowing the lawns, composting, that sort of thing. And it is no good looking at me like that. The fact is we are both set in our ways and will always be good friends as long as we are both allowed our own space. Sharing is not an option.'

'But are you not lonely?'

'Lonely? With all my lovely plants?'

But, she reflected, those plants were so demanding.

8

I really wanted to come and join you on the working party the Monday after we met. It was too soon to rearrange my other jobs, but I was also nervous of meeting all your friends. They'd find out how little I knew about plants and things, and might ask me what I did. I didn't want to let myself down. Actually it was you I didn't want to let down.

Ken eased the nose of his Focus up against the wire fence dividing the car park off from the west meadow. It was a lovely day, the silvery Swedish birch, dating from Ellen Willmott's day, rising from a carpet of yellow; the purple crocuses showed on the other side of the drive, in the east meadow.

He waved to some of the early arrivals as he made his way to the rear of his car and opened the tailgate. Several were already decked out in boots, gloves and an assortment of coats. Not so much protection from the cold on a day like this, but more to guard against the thorns, splinters and other perils which in unguarded moments they could come across before they were done.

After pulling on the big socks, he slipped his right foot into his boot and tied the laces tight. The left one was more of a problem since a combination of stiff leather badly in need of softening and a foot that was slightly larger than his right one made the operation sometimes just a little painful. Any aches soon wore off as the leather warmed up, so a grunt as he heaved the boot up and tied the laces was the only outward sign of any difficulty.

'Hello Ken, good to see you.'

'Oh, hi Daphne,' he said. 'Full house this morning.'

'Yes,' she said, glancing at the line of cars. 'Must be the weather that's brought everyone out. Frank and Ben will be pleased. I think Frank is going to cut down a couple of sycamores so no doubt we'll have some logs to fetch and split.'

Frank, the warden, and his assistant Ben both worked tirelessly to keep Warley Place a safe and attractive wildlife refuge and one of the plants that would take over given half a chance was the sycamore. Other plants such as bamboo, Himalayan balsam, giant hogweed and the like had mostly been either eradicated or reduced to manageable proportions, but were lurking there waiting for a chance to explode upon the reserve given half a chance.

Ken glanced towards the driveway as a movement caught his eye, but it was an early visitor walking in.

'The young lady you were with yesterday seemed very pleasant,' said Daphne. 'You suit each other.'

Oh God, was he that transparent?

'Have you known her long?'

'No,' said Ken. 'I hadn't met her before. She seemed a bit lost so I asked if she was all right. She wasn't, not really, so I took her round. Well, part of the way round, anyway.'

'I suppose she's working, otherwise she would be good to have in our team. It would be great to have some more young people.'

'Yes, I believe she is, but she said she might be able to reorganise things and join us.'

He wished he'd been a bit more positive about her coming, but he didn't want to be too pushy. Anyway, she'd probably got other commitments.

'Hi Ken,' called Gordon, coming over towards him. Gordon was the wag of the group, always making dreadful puns and seeing the funny side in everything. It was strange how much the group differed in their attitudes, experience, interests, talents, ages and just about everything else, but how well they got on together. Perhaps they got on *because* they were so different, Ken wondered.

'I gather some of us are going to be pushing the cart,' said Gordon. 'Frank's cutting down another sycamore and there's one he and David have already cut up, so we're going to be busy.'

'Right,' called out Ben, the assistant warden. 'We need four for the cart.'

Gordon and Ken bent down behind Ken's car, doing up their laces again. Pulling the cart loaded with logs was very strenuous work, even when going only slightly uphill.

'I think Gordon and Ken are over there,' said Norman, pointing to the car. 'And Peter is behind the shed looking at the leaf mould, and Donald is behind that tree.'

'I don't know what we'd do without you Norman,' said Ben, grinning from ear to ear. 'Especially for pulling the cart.'

'Actually I don't mind working on the cart,' said Norman, 'but my back's playing me up this morning.'

Gordon and Ken came out from behind the car, bent forward and holding their backs.

'Frank's got the key to the cart,' said Ben, taking no notice whatsoever of their playacting. 'The logs are up by the North hide.'

'Oh no,' groaned Gordon. 'Uphill whichever way we take it. Isn't this discrimination Ben?'

'What?'

'Us men always pulling the cart. The women will resent it and accuse us of sexual discrimination. I think we ought to let them do it.'

'Unfortunately the women have already got other jobs. Sorry.'

The four of them wandered up the drive towards the house. Strange that, the way they still called it the house even though it had been pulled down before the war. All except the conservatory, that is.

The cart was kept chained to a tree opposite, in what used to be the lawn area. There was a steep incline from the hide to the nearest point to which they could push it, so the logs would have to be manhandled up a dozen or so steps for loading. The path rose from there to the top of the hill where the house used to stand, but by taking a more circuitous route it would be at a less steep angle – steep enough, though, to pose a real challenge to those pushing it, particularly if the ground was soft.

Donald unlocked the chain and he and Peter pulled it out on to the path and down towards the North hide.

'I gather you managed to find yourself a nice young lass to go round with yesterday,' said Gordon.

'Oh, Elsie, yes,' said Ken. 'She'd never been before and was a bit nervous so I walked part of the route with her.'

There was silence for a bit.

'You're not going to tell us any more then?' asked Peter.

'What else is there to tell?' said Ken as the cart bounced over some tree roots.

'Sounds very suspicious to me,' said Gordon, steering it round a corner.

'Nothing suspicious at all,' grinned Ken. 'There's just nothing else to tell.'

'I saw you with her yesterday,' said Donald. 'I wish I were forty years younger, then I'd have tried to get in first. Is she coming again?'

'I don't know.'

'Didn't you ask?'

'Blimey you lot are worse than a load of women.'

He hadn't got a phone number or an address, so there wasn't much he could do about it now.

They parked the cart and started down the steps to the hide.

'Oh God!'

That was Gordon, on seeing the pile of logs already cut up and stacked by the side of the path. David had put one of the larger ones on its end and was already busy with the axe, splitting it into burnable pieces. As they watched the blade came plunging down and went through the log like a knife through butter. A splinter flew past, just missing Gordon.

'If anyone gets hit in the mouth will that be accidental damage?' asked Gordon.

'Well it would hardly be deliberate,' said Norman, who had tagged on behind the group when Ben couldn't think of anything suitable for him to do.

'It's just one of Gordon's puns,' said David. 'Just ignore it.'

'Pardon?'

'Axe-i-dental' explained David. 'Axe. Dental, mouth.'

'Oh. Right. I see.'

'If you stop for a moment we'll load the cart up,' suggested Peter.

'Can't see Elsie doing this,' commented Donald as he lifted an armful of logs and staggered up the steps to the cart.

'Me neither,' said Gordon as he dropped his load in. 'Don't suppose we'll see her again.'

'No, shouldn't think so,' said Peter as they walked back down for another load.

'Who's Elsie?' asked Norman.

'No one you know,' said Ken. 'Just a young woman I showed round yesterday. On the other hand she might have been your great granddaughter I suppose.'

'But I haven't got a great granddaughter. I'm not old enough.'

'Right, the cart's full enough,' said Donald. 'Any more and we won't get it up the slope.'

Donald and Peter grabbed the big handle at the front and the other two heaved at the back, the big soft tyres gradually turning as the contraption slowly wound its way up towards the walled garden.

'Good grief, how many barrow-loads do you think it'll take?' gasped Gordon.

'Depends how hard we push,' said Peter. 'If we really work at it we should get two more loads before tea.'

'Right,' said Gordon. 'We'd better slow down then!'

'Hang on a minute,' said Norman as he moved a piece of path edging for them, 'I'm not old enough to have a great granddaughter.'

'Oh, really?' said Ken. 'I smell smoke. Some lucky buggers are doing the bonfire.'

By the time they reached the flat ground by the conservatory they were all in need of a rest and leaned on the sides of the cart watching three others feeding brash on the flames of a huge fire opposite. One of them looked up, grinned and came ambling over.

'Might have known you'd get a cushy job,' remarked Peter.

'At my age it's all I can manage,' Robin said, trying hard to look contrite. 'Anyway, remember we were talking last week about digital clocks.'

'Yes,' said Donald. 'Whether if we all went digital the word 'clockwise' would have any meaning.'

'Right. Well I dug up a word that we could use instead. Widdershins.'

'Widder what? How do you spell it?'

Robin dutifully spelled it out.

'It means "in a direction contrary to the sun's course. Anticlockwise". There's another word, "deasil", that is the reverse, clockwise.'

'You really are a mine of useless information,' laughed Gordon.

63

'Ah, not useless,' said Robin. 'Going widdershins is unlucky. It's rumoured that if you walk three times round a church widdershins, you will see the devil looking at you from the porch!'

'Or three times round the bonfire widdershins and you'll see Ben looking at you from the conservatory asking you to get a move on with the logs,' suggested Donald.

'I don't believe in bad luck,' said Norman, promptly marching off to the bonfire and walking round it anticlockwise. Having completed three circuits he turned to them and shouted 'See?' before tripping over a pile of leaves and falling on to his back.

When the others had finished laughing Donald turned to Robin.

'Of course widdershins is only anticlockwise in the northern hemisphere,' he noted. 'It goes the other way in the south. And of course in the equatorial regions it changes from one direction to the other.'

'Hmmnnn... I'll have to think about that,' said Robin.

'Oh well, it's down hill now,' said Peter as they once more put their shoulders to the cart and it gradually picked up speed on its way to the car park where the logs were stored.

What a shame Elsie couldn't make it, thought Ken as he let go of the cart, leaving Gordon to guide it down the slope. Obviously she had a job and it was far too soon for her to make other arrangements for Monday morning, even if she had said she'd probably be able to. Pity he didn't have her telephone number, too, or her address. Maybe next Monday.

'By the way,' gasped Donald as he started to pull on the back to slow it down. 'I saw someone who seemed to be following you yesterday. Did you know him?'

'Oh yes,' said Ken. 'I knew him.'

9

There's so much history to Warley Place, isn't there? I'm sure we'll never know about most of what went on, but I bet there was a lot of thieving. It must have been so easy to get in, what with all those trees and shrubs, and fences that could be climbed over. I wonder if any of the people that did it felt sorry afterwards?

'You sure the old bat's away?' whispered Wally as they crept down Dark Lane, the narrow road that ran along the western perimeter of Warley Place.

It was dark, very dark, and Alfie felt a pang of fear as the high hedges to either side momentarily reminded him of the trenches he had inhabited not so long ago. Once they got through them the half moon, brushing the tree tops in the distance, would help them on their way but also make them more easily visible to others abroad this late at night. But not to be shot at, he reminded himself.

'I told you already,' he replied wearily, wishing he had never agreed to this. Spouting off about how mean she was, that was one thing, but actually stealing from her was different. 'Anyway, it's nearly midnight, she'd have been in bed long since.'

'Pity really. I'd like to teach her not to mess with Wally Barnes.'

He was quiet for a moment.

'So there's no one in the house?'

'No Wally, don't even think about it. Robinson often sleeps there when she's away. He won't just look the other way if he hears you. Willmott would suspect him, or more likely the day servants, if anything was missing when she came back, and sack them on the spot. Anyway – '

Wally's wife had let it slip that after his last attempt at stealing Ellen Willmott's plants he had come home with his trousers still wet, the result of meeting the formidable owner of Warley Place unexpectedly. He'd never lived that down, but woe betide anyone who reminded him of it. Alfie decided not to put it to the test.

'This'll do, we can get through the holly here.'

'I ain't getting scratched to bits by no holly.'

'It's a smooth-leaved holly,' said Alfie, sighing. '*Ilex aquifolium* 'Laurifolia'. It's got no spines, it won't hurt you.'

'Don't get smart with me,' spat Wally as he followed Alfie. 'Er... is it rare?'

'Do you mean is it valuable?'

'That too.'

'It's not common, but not particularly valuable. Anyway, I can't see you propagating it somehow.'

'Not me, but my customer might.'

'Forget it. Wrong time of year.'

'What's special about it?'

'Look, forget it. It doesn't bear any fruit but its flowers smell nice.' He sniffed. 'Not like you.'

'I warned you, don't get clever with me.'

'OK, but just leave it and concentrate on what we came for.'

Alfie guided Wally through the branches after pushing a rotting fence post down and they stood at the edge of the west meadow.

'She'll guess who took the plants, you know,' said Alfie, still hoping that Wally would change his mind.

'Yeah, but she'll never prove it. Not unless someone tells her. And you're not likely to do that, are you Alfie boy. After all, it was you what put me up to it!'

'No it wasn't,' protested Alfie.

The moonlight glinted on what was left of Wally's teeth as he grinned.

'We'd best go round the edge close to the trees,' said Alfie. 'Just in case Jacob is on the prowl, or the old girl's got the police to look in.'

'Police? You said nothing about police.'

'You never know with her,' said Alfie. 'It's not too late to go back.'

'Forget it. I've made promises to too many people. I owe them.'

'Oh.'

Alfie gave up. Best get on with it.

'Right, quiet now,' he whispered. 'Sound travels a long way at night. And bend double, then if anyone does see they'll think we are deer.'

Eventually, Wally puffing like a steam engine, they reached the top of the slope and came to a row of trees.

'Spanish chestnuts,' whispered Alfie.

'Can we take them?'

'Of course not, you can see they're enormous.'

'Exactly. So I'm not interested. Trees are trees. Shut up about them.'

'We're at the back of the walled garden,' said Alfie quietly. 'No one in the house will see us from here, but they might from the coach house when we turn the corner, so keep very quiet.'

There was a muffled curse from Wally as he tripped over a tree root.

They rounded the corner.

'What's that?' said Wally.

'Sh! It's a hothouse.'

'We can nick something from there.'

'Yes, we could. And they would all be dead by the time you got them to your mates. We're going to the nursery beds.'

They crept quietly along the side of the hothouse.

'This is the really tricky bit,' whispered Alfie. 'We have to cross in front of the coach house. It'll probably be OK, they'll all be asleep, but they'll wake if we disturb the horses. Just in case be very quiet and follow me.'

He shuddered as Wally tripped on a plant pot. If it was this difficult unladen, what would it be like when they were carrying bags of plants?

They crossed behind the coach house, hearing the horses stirring nervously, then edged their way by the horse pond.

'This is it,' said Alfie. 'This is where her plants are put to harden up and plant on. We can take some and get out of here.'

'Which are the valuable ones?'

'I don't know.'

'Corse you bloody know. Now which ones?'

'I don't have much to do with what goes on round here. All of them, I suppose. She wouldn't bother with them in a nursery otherwise.'

'Right, we'll take the labels too, then I can tell my mates what they are.'

'That won't do you much good. The special plants are labelled in her code. She does it when she hybridises them.'

'She what's them?'

'Hybridises. It means – '

'I don't give a shit what it means. Except that it means I'll give my mates plants and won't be able to tell them what they are. They'll be able to sell them like hot cakes. "These plants are REALLY special, so special even we don't know what they are." The customers will certainly fall for that!'

'Quiet, for gawd's sake Wally. Someone will come.'

Wally leered at him.

'I'm ready for them if they do.'

He slid a wicked looking knife, about a foot long, out of his boot.

Alfie froze.

Wally grinned and pushed it back in again.

'Right, let's get on with it then.' He produced a sack from his bag. 'We'll take what we can and sell them as whatever it says on the label.'

Alfie's stomach sank. If that wasn't a dead give-away as to where they had come from, nothing was.

'Who's there?'

They both sank down, their eyes peering into the darkness.

'That's Jacob,' whispered Alfie. 'He must have seen us from his cottage as we crossed the meadow. He's got a sixth sense about this place; knows all the noises, them that should be here and them that shouldn't.'

'He's her majesty's favourite gardener, ain't he?'

'Yes, her alpine garden depends entirely on him. She couldn't do without him.'

'Well she's going to have to.'

Alfie gasped as Wally drew his long knife again.

'No, don't, he's done you no harm. He's a good man.'

'It's even better than getting her,' Wally muttered to himself. 'She'll know why but she'll never prove it.'

He started to crawl towards the voice.

Alfie grabbed Wally's foot to hold him back and suddenly there was the knife blade an inch from his nose.

'Do that again and I'll stick you too!'

Alfie let go and Wally waited, knife at the ready.

'He might go away.'

They heard the crunch of approaching footsteps, much closer now.

Alfie reached forward to crawl ahead and warn Jacob, knowing that he would never make it. He felt Wally grab his coat and pull him back and felt the sharp point of the knife press against his ribs. His hand touched an old brick, fallen away from the edging of the nursery bed. Closing his fingers round it, scared stiff both for himself and for Jacob, he picked it up and swung his arm round.

He felt sick as he felt and heard the crunch of the brick hitting Wally's head.

Wally wouldn't be thieving or murdering tonight. Nor any other night, he suddenly realised.

10

*I was so worried about what your mum and dad would think
about me. I expected they would think I was a bit common and not
good enough for you. If so, I thought they would be right. That's
why I really decided not to go to Warley again. Until you rang,
that is. I'm so glad you rang.*

'Hi Mum, I'm back,' called Ken as he let himself in after kicking
his shoes off in the porch alongside his boots and rucksack.

'Something to eat?'

'No thanks, I've had my sandwiches. I'll just have a shower.'

'You seem a bit down. Are you OK?'

'I'm fine. Did you enjoy the art class?'

His mother was more enthusiastic than talented, but did some
passable watercolours when she put her mind to it.

'Yes thanks Ken. I'm improving, but slowly.'

'See you in a minute then.'

He went though to the bathroom, peeled off his dirty clothes
and dumped them in the washing basket. She was right; he did
feel a bit down. He hadn't really expected that Elsie would be
there, but couldn't help hoping. There was something special
about her; something that attracted him. Perhaps it was her wish
for something better; not money, that was plain, but something
more out of life. He guessed that it was difficult for her at home
and that her work was humdrum. She was pretty, but it wasn't
just that. Best to forget her, he tried to convince himself as he
stepped into the cleansing spray. Mind you, some people were
wondering why he didn't have a steady girlfriend by now, or was
married even. The truth was that he simply hadn't met anyone
that he'd want to spend the rest of his life with. That, and the fact
that some of the girls he'd been out with didn't like him working
weekends when they were off, or going to college and some
nights studying.

A few minutes later, clean and dry, wearing fresh clothes and
holding a copy of an Ian Rankin novel, he made his way back
downstairs.

'Cup of tea then?' his mother asked as he poked his head round the kitchen door.

'Thanks.'

'Was she there then?'

He wished he hadn't said anything yesterday, but couldn't stop himself. Now they wanted to know everything when there was nothing much to tell.

'No, but she works during the week.'

'What does she do?'

'No idea, I didn't ask.'

'Oh.'

'Don't interrogate the boy,' came a gruff voice from the lounge.

'Oh, hi dad, didn't know you were in.'

'Had enough work for now. They can get on well enough without me. In fact I think they'd rather I stayed out of the way!'

Ken went in to the spacious lounge. It was at the rear of the house, looking out on to a large garden laid out with the best of the plants, shrubs and trees taken from one of their nurseries. They weren't strictly speaking 'their' nurseries, they were his father's, but it had been taken for granted that one day they would be his. They would have been his sister Marion's too, if she hadn't died so young.

His father had worked honestly and hard for his money and liked the good things in life. The carpet was thick, the four piece suite deep and comfortable, the pictures on the walls all originals. One of them, a bunch of daffodils in a vase, was something his mother had painted recently and his father had insisted on framing it and having it on show. Ken chuckled as he remembered Mrs Barlow coming in from next door one day. She fancied herself as a bit of an art expert and she had frowned when she noticed it hanging there. Then when she saw the signature she had turned, smiled, and said how good it was.

Although the garden centre had been a family business for many years, it was very run down when he took over and he had built it up in a very competitive market. The risks he had taken along the way had paid off, but it could easily have been otherwise.

'Good morning?'

71

'Carting logs, so tiring and a bit boring, but good company as usual.'

'Right. Keeps you fit too I suppose.'

'I keep fit enough working for you!' said Ken, not unkindly. His father made sure that his son wasn't given all the soft jobs. He had to work his way up and wouldn't have wanted it any other way. It would be difficult enough to take over when the time came and he needed to prove himself to the managers who ran things so efficiently at the moment.

'You'll be running out of sycamore trees eventually.'

'I hope so,' grinned Ken, settling back into an armchair. 'Pushing that cart really does me in.'

'Can't they get a tractor or something?'

Ken turned his head to his mother as she stood in the doorway waiting for the kettle to boil.

'No, there's nowhere safe to put it. I wish there was.'

'What do the women do while you're doing the hard work pushing that thing?'

'Other sorts of hard work. Laying bricks, pulling bracken, clearing leaves, all sorts of things.'

'Is that what Elsie – was that her name? – would be doing?'

'I expect so. I don't organise the work, Frank and Ben do.'

'Donald hasn't found anything else in the walls?' asked his father.

Ken wasn't sure which was worse, his mother's relentless quest for information about Elsie that he didn't have, or his father's complete silence on the subject.

'I don't think so,' said Ken. 'All that happened before I joined and apart from the occasional comment they don't talk about it much.'

A year or so ago Donald had found a journal hidden in a wall he was renovating, leading to a discovery about a pilot from the First World War who had ended up at Warley Place having lost his memory.

Ken opened his book.

'Why don't you ask Elsie round for tea?'

'Mum, for all I know she won't come again,' he said.

'All right, I'll let you read your book.'

Ken waited for the inevitable follow-up question, but when it didn't come he started reading again.

'Why don't you ask her anyway?'

Ken sighed and put his book down.

'Because I don't know where she lives. Any more questions?'

'It was only a suggestion. What did you say she did?'

'I didn't say because I don't know. You asked me that earlier.'

'So I did. Sorry.'

'She doesn't work in horticulture, I know that. She isn't familiar enough with plant names. But she loves flowers. Animals and trees too, but flowers in particular.'

'She sounds nice.'

'She's not from a wealthy family though.'

'Oh.'

'Thank God for that,' his father interjected. 'Now shall I get the thumbscrews? That's about the only way you'll get any more information out of him.'

'What does she look like?'

'Mum, I'd like to read my book. All right, she's about twenty years old.'

He waited.

'And?'

'I was waiting for you to tick it off your list.'

'No need to be like that. I just want to know what sort of girl my son is going out with.'

'I'm not going out with her.'

'But you'd like to. So what else?'

'She's medium height, a bit over one and a half metres.'

'Ken, you know –'

'Sorry,' he grinned. 'Five foot five or six. Long black hair. Nice oval face, large eyes. Quite slim.'

'How slim?'

'Very slim. But she still has a figure.'

'Right.' Her eyes clouded over. 'I'll go and get the tea.'

He felt his father's eyes looking at him.

'Yes dad, she is like Marion,' he said. 'But she's not anorexic, just slim.'

His sister Marion's death was still a raw wound. They all privately thought that they could have done more to help her

73

through the eating disorder that had finally killed her, and nothing the doctor or the counsellor could say would convince any of them otherwise.

'It will be hard for your mother.'

'I know. She'll either like her or hate her.'

'Only one way to find out. Bring her over. Not for tea, nothing formal, just drop in on the way somewhere. She'll feel more at ease then.'

'Thanks dad. I will.'

He sat there for a while staring at his book.

'Go on lad, ring her.'

'I don't know if she has a phone.'

'Find out.'

'OK dad, you're right.'

He thought for a moment. Daphne kept all the details of volunteers but Elsie wasn't yet a volunteer, even though Ken hoped she soon would be. He picked up the local telephone book and his heart sank when he saw the number of Clarks listed, not to mention Clarkes.

Rummaging around in a drawer he found the local Brentwood map and opened it out. Then painstakingly he went through all the Clarks, making a cross against them if their address was anywhere near where he had dropped her off.

After about fifteen minutes there were six crosses. One of them was quite close, the rest a little further away.

Taking a deep breath he entered the number, hoping it was the right one and if so that it would be Elsie and not her father who answered the phone. Suddenly realising that she would be at work he was about to replace the handset when the ringing tone stopped and a voice came answered. His heart beat a little faster. It was her.

'Hello?'

A tentative, slightly nervous voice, as if she was expecting bad news.

'Hi Elsie. It's Ken, from Warley Place.'

'Oh, hello. Sorry I couldn't make it this morning but – '

'Don't worry. We missed you, but you had said it would be difficult. Can I finish our walk round with you some time?'

'That would be lovely.'

'Now?'

'Oh dear. Sorry, I'm just going out and I can't really put it off. When else would be convenient?'

Was she giving him the brush off? She sounded genuinely sorry.

'Tomorrow?'

'Tomorrow. Yes, why not? What time?'

She sounded pleased.

'Any time you want. My father is pretty tolerant with me. During the day or evening, whenever you can make it.'

There was a pause.

'The morning would be best. About ten.'

'Fine, I'll pick you up at ten.'

'No, that's all right, I can make my own way.'

'Elsie, I'll pick you up. I know where you live. I'm looking forward to it.'

'I'll meet you on the corner of – '

'No,' he said firmly. He didn't know her house, but he knew the area and guessed why she didn't want him there. 'I'll be outside your house at ten.'

There was silence.

'Elsie.'

'Yes?'

'I'm so glad you're coming.'

He put the phone down.

'She's coming?'

'Well she's coming to Warley Place to finish the walk we started yesterday. I'll ask if she'd like to come back here afterwards.'

'Has she got far to come?'

He hadn't noticed his mother come back in to the room.

'No.' He took a deep breath. 'She lives in Brick Street.'

There was a silence, then 'Brick Street, that estate...'

'Yes mum. That estate.'

'Are you sure you know what you are doing?'

'Mum, you've not even met her but you're judging her already. She's pretty; she's interesting to talk to; she loves flowers and the nice things of life. I like her.'

'Ken's right,' broke in his father. 'Let's wait until we've seen her. Even then, she's Ken's choice, not ours.'

'I know that. But we can give him some advice, can't we? Best not wait until, well, you know, it's too late.'

'Mum,' said Ken exasperatedly, 'she hasn't tried to drag me off into the bushes you know. Mind you, if she did...'

'Ken! I'm only saying, some lads have had their futures ruined by being trapped like that.'

'And some women have had their futures ruined for the same reason.'

A loud click announced that the kettle had boiled and his mother went back to the kitchen.

'She's only worried for you Ken.'

'I know, but she hasn't even met her.'

'Yes, but at your age the hormones make you see things in an over-simplistic way. You want to have children, to procreate, and someone pretty comes along. It can be as simple as that. There must be plenty of women of your own sort of background.'

'Good grief, you're at it too now dad. You'll both be driving me to do the very thing you're trying to stop.'

'OK Ken. Just be careful and think about what you are doing. Right?'

'Right. By the way, Sam has been showing his face there a bit. In fact Elsie wondered who he was.'

'You didn't say anything, did you?'

'No, only that he was a nuisance.'

'Best keep it that way.'

Although Warley Place is magically beautiful, even in its current state, there is a sadness about it too, isn't there? You told me about that World War One pilot, Alex, and I know that the whole estate went to ruin on Ellen Willmott's death, so I suppose both those things play a big part in its history, but I feel there are other things too; sad things.

'I am glad to see you back Miss Willmott,' said Jacob Maurer standing and straightening his back from tending to his beloved Alpines.

'Perhaps you will not be so glad when you see the list I have before me,' said Ellen Willmott. 'But at least the walnut tree has been buttressed.'

'We have not been idle in your absence.'

'I have no doubt that you have worked hard Jacob. Whether all your staff have done the same is open to conjecture.'

Jacob sighed. When Ellen Willmott disappeared to her properties in France and Italy it was usually for a month, but it was unusual for her to travel at this time of the year even to Spetchley Park. What was not unusual was for her to produce a list of items needing attention the day following her return.

It was becoming obvious to everyone that her finances were insufficient to meet her needs – or rather her wants, Jacob felt – and she may well have gone to see to some aspect of the rumoured sale of her overseas properties. Certainly if she had dispensed with them some time ago, or better still not bought them in the first place, life would have been easier for her. Not so for her staff, for her absences brought welcome, albeit temporary, relief for them.

'Shall we examine the tree then?'

'As you wish, Miss Willmott.'

Jacob followed his employer to the bridge, both pausing briefly to look at the *Primula sikkimensis* growing by the large stone adjacent to the bridge over the gorge, then down the steep slope to the main drive.

'You keep my alpines well Jacob,' she remarked in a rare display of appreciation.

They were both a little breathless by the time they reached the top of the slope and stood for a moment looking at the walnut tree. A rattling noise behind caused them to turn.

'That's Stephen Townsend's Austin Vitesse,' she muttered. 'I wonder what the good doctor wants. And he has a passenger, a policeman from the look of him.'

'Perhaps one of the staff has been drinking a little too much of a night,' suggested Jacob.

'You are looking well Miss Willmott,' said Dr Townsend, stopping his car in the turning circle and dismounting.

'You too Doctor. It's been some time since you graced us with your presence.'

'Too long I fear. Please forgive the intrusion, but I have brought Inspector Rawlins with me. He has been asking about the man Alex who was once in your employ and I suggested that if you and I both spoke to him it would clear the matter once and for all.'

'But I spoke to the military about him many months ago. I do not know where he went, only that he was in a very agitated condition.'

'I regret having to bother you with this madam,' said Inspector Rawlins. 'Sadly the communication between us and the army is hampered by some files being of a confidential nature. All I require is for you to say what you just have, and now that you have done, once I have cleared another little matter I will be on my way. His details, such as they are, will be on our files as a missing person but I am afraid there is little hope of finding him if he does not wish to be found.'

'And what little matter is that?'

Inspector Rawlins climbed down from the car.

'A local man has disappeared,' he said. 'Some might be relieved at that, but we do have to investigate the matter. He is probably lying drunk somewhere and will unfortunately turn up again.'

'When did he disappear?'

'Two days ago.'

'I was at Spetchley Park then so there is little point in asking me anything. But why ask me anyway? I would hardly be familiar with such a man.'

A smile crossed the policeman's face.

'He is a man who apparently has on at least one occasion been caught attempting to steal from your gardens. You gave him quite a scare I believe.'

'Ah. I think I know who you mean, but I have not seen him since. He certainly looked a scoundrel.'

'We believe that he was intending to make a further attempt on your gardens a few days ago. His name is Barnes. Wally Barnes.'

'The name means nothing to me. What about you Jacob?'

'No, it means nothing to me either.'

'Was anything missing from the nursery beds or hothouses?'

'Nothing.'

'Well there you are Inspector. Now either I can get someone to show you round the estate so that you can satisfy yourself that nothing is amiss, or you can join the doctor and myself in the conservatory for a glass of lemonade.'

'The conservatory sounds the best option madam, you are most kind. If – I'm sorry, I don't know your name?'

'Jacob Maurer. I look after the Alpine garden.'

'If you, Mr Maurer, could ask your staff if they know of this man's whereabouts and let me know if anyone knows anything?'

'They are my staff,' said Ellen Willmott. 'However you may do as the Inspector asks, Jacob.'

'Certainly. May I go back to my work now?'

'You may.'

They walked slowly to the conservatory, Inspector Rawlins showing some horticultural knowledge as he admired several of the plants on the way.

'A fine room,' he said as his eyes roved round the interior of the room. 'A fine mahonia, too.'

'Please sit down,' said Ellen Willmott, motioning to a chair by a small table and sitting herself. Dr Townsend sat alongside the Inspector.

'That's two people connected to this estate, both missing; this chap Barnes, who is no great loss, and that other chap last year.... what was his name?'

'I think you know his name very well,' said Ellen Willmott. 'We knew him as Alex, which is the name Dr Townsend gave him.'

The Inspector had the grace to look embarrassed.

'Ah, thank-you Robinson,' she continued as her butler brought in the drinks. 'To save the Inspector asking, could you tell him what you know about Alex and a local thief called Barnes?'

'None of us knew much at all about Alex,' Robinson confirmed. 'But we miss him. He was a real gentleman. As for Barnes, I have never heard of him. I do not make a habit of acquainting myself with local rogues and vagabonds.'

'No, I didn't imagine for one moment that you would,' said the Inspector. 'Thank-you anyway.'

Ellen Willmott was silent. She missed Alex more than she would admit to anyone other than perhaps Robinson and Jacob, and probably not even to them.

'In my experience when someone goes missing their nearest and dearest pester us continually,' said the Inspector. 'They want to know if we have heard anything, what we are doing about it, that sort of thing. Funnily enough the people who in normal times desire to see us least suddenly bother us the most.'

'It must be very irritating for you, keeping you from your real work,' said Ellen Willmott.

'No, not really. One can understand why they do it. Our duty is to serve the public, who after all pay our wages. Well, some of them do, anyway.'

'If you are wondering why I do not pester you about Alex,' Ellen Willmott said pointedly, 'then I must say that I assume that either you or certainly Dr Townsend would immediately inform me of his whereabouts. There is little point in bothering you unnecessarily.'

She stared at the Inspector, her eyes crackling.

'Yes, quite. We appreciate that. Well, time we were going doctor?'

'Actually I have some further business with Dr Townsend,' she continued. 'If you ask Robinson he will arrange for someone to drop you off at your next destination.'

'This way sir,' said Robinson appearing from nowhere and ushering the policeman out towards the coach house.

'You really were fond of Alex, weren't you?' said the doctor.

'Yes, he was a good man. Almost a son to me, the son I never had.'

'Please tell me to mind my own business if you wish, but have you never thought about a family?'

'It's far too late for that,' she said softly.

'But not too late to have a man in your life; someone to share things with; worries, pleasures, your music, your garden?'

'But who would want to? Probably only someone who wanted an easy ride through the rest of his life, I suspect.'

'You have a very cynical view of life Ellen.'

'Perhaps. But if someone of a strong character were to enter my life then we would always be arguing. If they were not of strong character I wouldn't want them.'

'You got on with Alex well enough.'

'Not in the way you are suggesting. Be honest, could you live with me?'

'I admit I have wondered from time to time, indeed hoped that we might become closer. But our interests would keep us apart even if we resided in the same house. My medical work, your garden, we are both obsessed in our own different ways.'

'But we get on well when we do see each other, don't we?'

'We do, and I hope we remain the best of friends Ellen,' he said.

12

I liked our second walk round Warley Place even more than the first. I was very nervous to begin with, frightened that I'd say the wrong thing. But I needn't have worried, need I? It really didn't matter, not to you. I was right to worry about your mum though, wasn't I? But your dad was lovely.

Ken turned into Brick Street with some trepidation. He couldn't but help notice the state of the small front gardens, the grey-looking net curtains, the suspicious eyes looking at him as he drove past. He knew which house was Elsie's without looking at the number. The paintwork was peeling just as much as the others; the front door and window frames needed replacing and the rotting wooden gate hung loose on one hinge, but the curtains were clean and un-creased and the small front garden was a picture of well balanced colour.

She came quickly out through the door as he pulled to a stop, closing it behind her and reaching the car almost before he had undone his safety belt. Instead of opening the passenger door from the inside, he got out and walked round to open it from the pavement.

She was wearing the same clothes as she had before, a yellow blouse and blue jacket, but he noticed that she had a new flowered skirt matching the rest of her clothing perfectly. Her long black hair had been brushed until it shone like water flowing over Whitby jet.

'You look nice,' he said.

She smiled.

'Have you brought your notebook? You might need it.'

'Oh. No, I haven't.'

She stood there.

'Go on, you'll regret it if you don't.'

'All right.' Then, turning back as she started up the path, 'I won't be a minute.'

Ignoring her unspoken plea not to, he followed her.

'Hello Mrs Clark,' he said as the door opened, 'I thought Elsie might need her notebook.'

'Pleased to meet you,' said Elsie's mother, taking his proffered hand. 'It's really good of you to pick Elsie up to show her round the gardens.'

'It's entirely my pleasure,' he said warmly.

'Right, I've got it,' said Elsie half running down the stairs.

'Have you got your sketches?'

'Mother!'

'She's done some nice drawings of the flowers. She don't like people to see them though. But you'd like them, I know you would.'

'I didn't know that. Yes, please Elsie, bring them too. We might see something there you can sketch. Oh, and you've got just the right shoes on for walking round the reserve, but if you want you could bring some others to change into afterwards in case they get muddy.'

Just as she disappeared upstairs again a figure appeared from the kitchen, trousers belted tightly under a beer belly; vest, but not yet a shirt above it, tucked into the trousers; unshaven face from which an overly red nose protruded just below bleary looking eyes partly visible below hair hanging down over his forehead.

'Hello Mr Clark,' Ken said.

The apparition disappeared.

Else came rushing down the stairs with shoes in one hand and an A5 spring-bound notebook in the other. Her eyes were open wide and her brow furrowed as she glanced towards the kitchen.

'See you later Mum,' she said.

'We'll eat out at the *Thatchers* if that's all right with you,' said Ken to both of them.

'You enjoy yourself,' said Mrs Clark. 'I'll see you when I see you.'

'I'm sorry,' said Elsie as they reached the car and Ken bent to open the door.

'What for?'

'My father, looking like that.'

'Lucky I'm not going out with your father then!'

She started to giggle.

'And your Mum is lovely.'

She turned to look at him and his heart melted. He reached out his arm and gave her a hug, then pretended not to notice the tears

83

in her eyes. Looking up he waved to her mother, smiling at them and waving back. Funny how people could smile and look happy but worried at the same time.

'What a lovely day for it,' Ken said as the car slid away from the kerb. 'I'm so glad you could come.'

'So am I,' said Elsie.

'Your mum looked pleased. She's nice, isn't she?'

'I think so. I'm sorry dad wasn't a bit more presentable or a bit more sociable, but that's what he's like.'

'He probably thinks I've taken you off to have my evil way with you,' he laughed.

'Oh dear, haven't you?' she giggled.

In just a few minutes they were pulling up outside the Warley Place main gate and Ken jumped out to swing it open. When he got back in Elsie was looking at the little cottage alongside the drive.

'I can't believe that the gardener lived there with nine children.'

'Jacob Maurer, yes. Four boys and five girls. The girls were all named after flowers.'

'How nice. What were they?'

'Ah, now you're asking! Rose, Lily and Violet, I remember them. And Iris. The other one was less common. Not Marigold, but like that.'

'Marguerite?'

'Yes, that's right, Marguerite.'

He slipped the car into gear and drove slowly up the drive.

'And what was their mother's name?'

'Rosina. She was from Switzerland, same as he was.'

'Poor woman. I bet she was homesick.'

'I don't know. No one seems to know much about her. She died very soon after she had her last child, Iris. TB I think.

'Oh no. How sad.'

He glanced at her face as he turned into the little car park; her brow furrowed, her mouth down and her eyes blinking. He wondered at the way she had immediately empathised with this woman she had never known.

Half a dozen other cars were already lined up against the wire fence and he guided the car between two of them.

She looked across the daffodils as she got out, smiling to herself.

'They're lovely aren't they,' he commented as he locked the doors. 'Even better from the other end of the meadow. It's lovely seeing you smile.'

She went to speak, then stopped.

'What is it?'

'You'll think I'm silly.'

'No, I promise not to laugh.'

'I was remembering when I came that first time and saw those daffodils.'

'There's nothing silly about that.'

'Well.' She hesitated. 'I wore my yellow blouse to match them, but I didn't see any at first and felt silly. Then when I saw those I was so relieved.'

'You are funny,' he laughed, taking her hand. 'As if anyone would notice even if they weren't out. But I know what you mean.'

They wandered through the inner gate and over to the pond to the left of the drive. They stood for a moment, looking at the moorhens.

'You know you said it was lucky you weren't going out with my father?' said Elsie hesitantly.

'Yes.'

'Does that mean you are going out with me? As opposed to just taking me round Warley Place?'

'Oh dear,' he said.

Her face dropped.

'No, that's not what I meant,' he hurriedly went on. 'It's just that, well, it's not exactly the most exciting place to take someone, is it? But yes, if you don't mind, I am taking you out.'

'At the moment it's the most exciting place in the world,' she said, lifting her face up towards him.

The next minute his arms were round her and hers round him. Their lips met in a long, long kiss.

Eventually they parted and resumed their stroll, arms round each other's waist.

'Can I ask you a question?' he said. 'You needn't answer it if you don't want to.'

'Anything.'

'You are beautiful. No boyfriend?'

'I like hearing you say it, but I'm not beautiful.' Ignoring his protest, she continued. 'You've seen where I live. I went out with Billy Hopkins once, but he only wanted one thing. He didn't get it and knew he was never going to so that was the end of him. Jamie Bowman has been given the same message but doesn't seem to have understood it. They all think I'm boring. I think they are. So no, I haven't got a boyfriend. Or at least I didn't have, not until today. And you?'

'Only you. I have seen other girls of course, but only briefly. I work Saturdays normally and most Sundays and they don't like that, and I just didn't see any future with any of them.'

He felt her muscles tense.

'Sorry, I'm being a bit premature talking about the future.'

'It's not that. It's just that... No, forget it. I'm happy with now. You may feel different about a future once you know me.'

He stopped walking and turned to her.

'What's bothering you? Best tell me now, then we can really enjoy ourselves.'

He saw water appearing in her eyes.

'I'm a cleaner,' she said, the tears trickling down her cheeks now. 'A cleaner. I work in an office, yes, but cleaning the bloody thing! Can you take me home now?'

He didn't say anything at first, just hugged her to him. Then, pulling out his handkerchief, he dabbed the tears from her face.

'What's wrong with being a cleaner?' he said. 'I don't care what you do to earn your keep, as long as it's honest work. I'm glad you've told me, but now forget it. I'm afraid in a few short days I've fallen in love with you.'

Oh God, was he being too forward?

'I fell in love with you the moment we met,' she said. 'Only I didn't think anything would come of it.'

They walked on, past the fallen lime tree, on up the path.

'Have you got any secrets?' she said.

'Not really. But you remember I said I worked in a garden centre?'

'Yes, I remember.'

'I do. And I do a lot of the grind. Serving the customers, humping stuff about, anything that needs doing as long as it doesn't need too much horticultural expertise. I'm going to college to learn that.'

'I wish I was doing something like that.'

'You might be able to. My dad owns several garden centres. They'll be mine one day.'

He saw her eyes shut and her brow crease. She didn't say anything for a bit, then,

'What are your mum and dad going to think of me?'

'They've both worked hard for what they've got. They'll understand, especially dad. Even if they didn't, I wouldn't care. I love you Elsie Clark.'

'I thought Sunday was special,' she said. 'Today even beats that.'

They reached the open area opposite the turning circle and turned to look at the walnut tree.

She shivered a little.

'Are you all right?' he asked anxiously. 'I'll run back and get a coat from the car.'

'No, I'm fine,' she assured him. 'It's just that there's something about that tree.'

'Well it's very old. Did I not tell you about it on Sunday?'

'You did mention it, yes, on the way back at the end of our walk.'

'Right. Well, as I think I said, it must have been quite old even in Ellen Willmott's time, because the trunk went a bit rotten and she had to fill it with concrete to stop it falling down.'

'Oh, I've never heard of anyone doing that before. It looks as though it should have a seat round it. I can imagine it with one.'

He looked at her in surprise.

'It did, in her ladyship's time before she did that to it. There's a photograph that shows it. How did you know?'

'I don't know. It just seemed right. Perhaps I saw the picture. But there's something about it. I can't explain. It must be just me.'

'Ben reckons we're going to have to renovate the concrete, probably in the next few weeks. The top is looking a bit wobbly so we'll have to get it off and refill it without harming the tree.'

Ken looked at his watch.

'We're going to have to do the full walk another time I think,' he said. 'I told mum and dad we'd drop in on the way home. If we go round the walled garden, then back by the gorge, that should give us time to fit everything else in.'

'See your mum and dad?'

Her eyes were wide, her forehead creased.

'Don't worry, they'll love you.'

His dad would, he knew that. He wasn't so sure about his mother. Best not to mention the cleaning, not just yet. Which said more about his mum than it did about Elsie, he realised.

Ken led her past the headache tree, reputed to bring on a headache if anyone crushed a leaf and smelled it, into the conservatory – or rather what used to be a conservatory. It was now just the brick and masonry remnants of the room in which Ellen Willmott used to sit and write or read when she wasn't gardening. Closed down for some time for safety, it had been stabilised at some considerable cost but was now open to the public. Open to the elements too, for it had no roof. They sat down on one of the benches and Ken took Elsie's hand in his.

'Ellen Willmott used to sit here,' he said. 'That was a lawn out there, and there was a rose arbour. Now there's just trees.'

'I can't imagine her holding someone's hand though,' said Elsie.

'No, me neither.'

'There was a mahonia growing against that wall,' commented Ken. 'Before the building work was done we took it up and replanted it. One or two people took parts of the root home and grew them.'

They sat there for a while before rising and moving on to the walled garden, where a group of seven or eight people were gathered together looking at one of the trees.

'Who are they?' whispered Elsie.

'That's the specialist gardening group,' said Ken. 'They walk round once a month to check on the plants, identify any rare ones and try to do something about any that look a bit dodgy. That's probably why they are looking at the Japanese large-leafed magnolia at the moment.'

'Do they know who you are?'

'Oh yes, I join them sometimes. It's good to learn about the plants. The only snag is that if you don't know the Latin names they get really annoyed, and if you can't identify the plants at all, well, they just stop speaking to you for the rest of the day.'

'Oh no, can we go somewhere else then,' pleaded Elsie.

'No, I'll introduce you to Deirdre. I'll have to, she's seen us. Pretend you are French and don't understand her, that's the best thing to do.'

'Ken, PLEASE can we go.'

Ken waved at Deirdre, who came towards them.

'I was only joking,' Ken whispered in Elsie's ear. They don't expect the likes of me to know anything at all. They are just pleased that we want to learn.'

'You beast,' spluttered Elsie. 'I'll get you for that when we're alone.'

'Can't wait,' laughed Ken as Deirdre came up to them. 'Hi Deirdre. I'm just showing Elsie round, otherwise I'd have been with you this morning.'

'Hello Elsie, pleased to meet you,' said Deirdre. 'I hope Ken is looking after you well?'

'Oh he certainly is. It's lovely here, isn't it?' replied Elsie. 'But there's so much I don't recognise.'

'There's a lot none of us would recognise without looking in our books,' Deirdre reassured her. 'Join us if you would like to?'

'I think they might want to be on their own,' smiled another lady, joining them.

'Hello Sally,' said Ken. 'This is Elsie. Yes, you're right, we won't join you today thanks. We will on another day, but this is only Elsie's second visit so we'll make our own way round. Trouble with the magnolia?'

'Yes, we think so,' said Deirdre. 'It doesn't look too healthy, does it? We managed to propagate a couple of new ones from seed last year so if they survive we might be glad of them.'

'Come on, we'll continue round now we are here,' said Ken to a doubtful Elsie as Deirdre and Sally made their way back to the group.

'The camellia is lovely, isn't it?' she said, relaxing as they walked on. 'And look at those magnolias.'

Her eyes were wide and sparkling now, not wide and frightened. They turned to go along the north wall.

'Don't know what they are,' said Ken, pointing to some yellow flowers. 'I ought to. I keep meaning to ask.'

'Lesser celandine,' said Elsie.

Ken was impressed. She must have been swotting up on her wildflowers.

'I'd have thought you'd have learned the names of all the flowers, what with working in a nursery and coming here one day a week,' teased Elsie.

'I should. I know most of the ones we sell in dad's place, but I feel embarrassed at keep asking what all the flowers are here. Still, now I've got you to tell me.'

Working their way past the roses on the west wall, they came to the southern-most one.

'This is where Donald found the journal a year or so ago,' said Ken. 'We keep looking for something else exciting, but all we find are old plant labels.'

'So you know exactly what plants she had growing here?'

'Well not always. Some of the labels have plant names on them, but others have a sort of code that we haven't deciphered yet and probably never will. Like the one you found in the orchard area. She couldn't have wanted other people to know, probably because they were special hybrids.'

They wandered out, hand in hand, turning to go up towards the Spanish chestnuts, also called Evelyn's chestnuts because it was said by Ellen Willmott that John Evelyn planted them in the seventeenth century. In front of the huge trees was a carpet of mossy grass.

'Do you know what they are?' asked Ken, pointing at some yellowy-white flowers that looked a bit like daffodils with the outer petals folded back.

'Aren't they Angel's Tears?'

'Damn! I come across something I know and you know it anyway. Oh well. It's a *Narcissus triandrus*, in case you want to know the Latin name.'

'You'll have to remind me later,' she said. 'I left my notebook in the car. I don't know that one though.'

She was looking at a bunch of big oval leaves in a clump, from which sprouted delicate lilac flowers.

'That's a Dog's-tooth violet,' said Ken. Except that it's not a violet, it's a member of the Lily family. *Erythronium dens-canis.* But don't ask me any more, that's exhausted my knowledge of wild flowers.'

They admired the view over a rather misty London and walked in silence.

'That's a funny name,' said Elsie looking at a notice by the path. "Persian ironwood tree." Which one is that?'

Ken pointed to a tree a little way off the path.

'It may have been planted there to indicate the beginning of perhaps the most outstanding part of the garden,' he said. 'The alpine garden.'

'It doesn't look anything special,' she said, her forehead creased.

'We shouldn't really do this,' Ken said. 'If visitors do it they might get hurt or damage some of the plants, but come on.'

He took her hand and helped her up a short slope until they were standing in front of a smallish tree.

'Look at the way those branches fuse together when they cross,' he pointed out. 'And look at that branch, starting off in one direction and reversing itself to go the opposite way.'

'That's weird,' she said excitedly. 'I've never seen anything like that before.'

'Come on,' he said taking her hand again. 'We'd better get down before any visitors see us and think they can do the same.'

They slid back down to the path, where Else went to pull out her notebook before remembering that she had left it in the car.

'*Parrotia persica,*' Ken spelled out. 'Don't worry, I'll remind you later.'

They walked on as the ground on their left changed to a deep ravine with large rocks on each side and by the path.

'These rocks are huge!' said Elsie, clambering up on top of a low slab-like one. 'How on earth did they get them here?'

'Careful,' warned Ken, 'they might be slippery. Labour was cheap in those days I suppose; although it's hard to imagine, even then. This is where Jacob Maurer spent most of his time.'

'Are you going to restore it?'

'Goodness me no, not as far as I know. These trees weren't here then, so they'd have to be cut down to let more light in. And there used to be a small stream running along the bottom, but there's no water at all running through now so we'd have to find that from somewhere. It would also take more care than we could give it. No, we just leave it to the imagination.'

He was tempted to take her over to see the filmy fern cave, built by Ellen Willmott to house her rare translucent ferns, but looked at his watch and decided against it.

'I'd like this to go on for ever,' he said, 'but do you mind if we get back? We can go for a walk later if you like. Or perhaps the pictures if you have the time?'

'That would be nice,' she said, squeezing his hand.

'I'll just let them know we're coming,' he said, letting go and taking his mobile phone from his pocket.

'I thought we were going to the *Thatchers*?'

'Oh yes. Do you mind if we have some soup or something at home instead?'

He saw her eyes widen.

'Then if you're hungry I'll take you out to eat this evening. Just us.'

'That would be lovely.'

They walked back down the path in silence, looking at the buds on the rhododendrons just showing their promise of things to come, even one or two clumps of very late snowdrops.

As they reached the main drive Elsie glanced back towards the house and stopped suddenly.

'All right?' asked Ken anxiously.

'Sorry, I'm imagining things.'

'What?'

'I just thought I saw someone. Remember that man we saw when I came here first?'

'Oh, him? Yes.'

'I could have sworn I saw him. Even if it was, he's gone now. He gives me the creeps.'

Ken started to walk in that direction but Elsie tugged at him.

'No, don't spoil today,' she said. 'It's been lovely.'

'I've enjoyed it too,' he said. 'You're right, I'll leave it.'

They wandered back to the car park.

Opening the passenger door for her he reached in and lifted out her notebook to jot down the name of the Persian ironwood tree for her. The sketchbook tumbled out too and fell open at a drawing of a snowdrop. He glanced at it before closing the cover.

'You can note down the Latin names of the other plants as we drive if you like,' he said, passing both to her before walking round to his side of the car.

They sat in contented silence as they drove towards Brentwood, but suddenly he pulled in to the side of the road.

'Sorry,' he said as she looked at him, puzzled. 'I just saw that parking space and thought you'd like to see something.'

He got out and opened the other door for her, then took her hand as they walked a short distance back the way they had come before turning down a short road.

'Lorne Road,' he said. 'It used to be Cemetery Road, but was renamed some time after the war – World War Two, that is. The cemetery isn't used now and it's kept as a nature reserve but the graves are mostly still cared for. Why are you laughing?'

'I'm sorry Ken,' she said. It's just that when we got here today you were worried because you thought taking me round Warley Place wasn't very exciting. But now we're going round a cemetery!'

He laughed. 'Oh my God,' he said. 'I see what you mean. But I think you'll understand why.'

'That's the old sexton's lodge,' he continued, pointing to his left before opening an old iron gate for her. 'It's the Brentwood Museum now, but it only opens one day each month and today isn't one of those days.'

'I never knew we had a museum,' she said as they walked through. 'I'd like to go in some time.'

'OK, if the excitement won't be too much for you,' he grinned as they continued down a path past a boarded up building.

'That used to be the little chapel,' he explained as they passed it. 'And that,' he continued as they reached a yew tree, 'is where Rosina Maurer is buried.'

'No gravestone?' she whispered.

'No. Lots of people in those days couldn't afford stones. I like to think Jacob planted this tree instead.'

They stood there, deep in thought, arms round each other's waist.

'Coming?' he said after a few minutes.

'Thank-you for bringing me here,' she said quietly as they turned and walked slowly back to the car.

They were nearing his home before he noticed her small hands clenched in her lap and, glancing at her face, the wide-open eyes.

'You're not worried about meeting my parents, are you?' he asked.

'A bit,' she admitted.

'There's only one thing you should perhaps know,' he said. 'Just in case the subject comes up. I had a sister who died a few years ago. Marion.'

'Oh, I am sorry.'

'She died as a result of anorexia. She looked very like you and it might bring back some memories, so if they are both a bit quiet you'll know why.'

'I can meet them another time,' she said hopefully.

'No, let's do it now, then it won't be hanging over you.'

They pulled into the drive of a large detached double-fronted house sitting a good twenty metres back from the road and came to a stop in front of a double garage to one side. The front garden was enormous, much bigger than most back gardens she had seen.

'Oh my God, is this your house?'

'I hope so, or the people that live there are going to get a shock when I let myself in!'

He saw her lips trying to form a smile as she took it in. Mostly close-cut lawn, with flower beds round the outside, shrubs dotted about and a large mimosa tree by the pavement, its yellow blossom fading now. What caught her attention though was a tree not yet in flower but with branches that bent in all directions and where crossing fused together at the joint.

'Is that what I think it is?' she asked.

'Yes, near the gorge, a Persian ironwood tree. *Parrotia persica*,' he reminded her. 'Just relax. They'll love you, the same as I do.'

'S'pose they want to know what I do?'

'Then we'll tell them. But they won't ask.'

'Hi mum, dad, it's me,' he called as he opened the front door. The net curtains in the lounge window had not quite fallen back into place, he had noticed as they walked up the path.

Ken suppressed a grin as his mother came busying in from the kitchen, wiping her hands on her apron.

'Hello dear, do come in. It's lovely to meet you after all Ken has told us.'

She held out her hand and shook Elsie's as Elsie smiled nervously and responded. For one awful moment Ken thought Elsie was going to curtsey when he saw her knees bend just very slightly. He saw his mother's eyes flick up and down his girlfriend's slim frame and knew that Elsie would have seen it too. At least she had some idea why.

'Good to see you Elsie.'

His father had come in from the garden, slipping off his boots at the back door and padding to them in his socks.

'Stephen, where are your slippers? Are you going to wash your hands?'

'Sorry dear, upstairs, couldn't wait to see Ken's young lady, and yes.'

'It's good to see you too Mr Bradshaw,' she said, responding to genuine warmth, while he washed his hands in the kitchen sink before feeling his firm grip in her own.

'Soup's ready,' said Stella Bradshaw, stirring a bubbling saucepan. 'I hope you like vegetable soup. It's home made, fresh from the garden.'

'It sounds lovely.'

'Come on through then Elsie,' said Ken's father, ushering her into the dining room. 'And it's Steve. Everyone calls me that.'

Ken pulled out a chair for her from the long polished table and sat next to her, unsure as to whether she knew which was her bread roll plate and which her glass but confident that she would follow him.

'The front garden is very pretty,' said Elsie as Mrs Bradshaw poured out the soup.

'I'm glad you like it. What do you think of the *Parrotia persica*?'

Ken grinned to himself as Elsie replied 'I'm not very good with trees, but I do like the way the branches all twist together and join up when they meet. It is the Persian ironwood tree, isn't it?'

'Yes, that's right. You prefer flowers then?'

'Yes. I was a bit lost at Warley Place though, with the trees and the flowers, there was a lot I didn't recognise.'

'Not surprised,' laughed Ken's father. 'Ellen Willmott got plants from all over the world. You'd have to be a real wizard to know them all.'

'What are your favourites then?' asked Mrs Bradshaw.

'It depends on the time of year. The daffodils are lovely when they are out, but I think I like snowdrops most of all.'

'Which variety?'

'Mother!' exclaimed Ken. 'You sound like one of those galanthophiles that come into our nursery.'

'What's a galanthophile?' asked Elsie.

'It's someone who is fanatical about snowdrops and likes boasting about the number of different varieties they've got, or even just seen somewhere. They couldn't actually tell the difference if they were put in front of them though.'

'Kenneth!' exclaimed his mother.

'Well,' he laughed. 'Most of them really are so alike you'd need an eyeglass to tell the difference, and then with difficulty.'

'The common one is lovely,' said Elsie. '*Galanthus nivalis*, isn't it?'

Ken saw a broad grin stretch across his father's face.

'Shall we let Elsie get on with her soup?' he suggested. 'We'll take a stroll round the back garden later if you like.'

'I'd like that very much,' said Elsie. 'This soup is very nice.'

'Help yourself to a bread roll.'

Ken smiled to himself as Elsie passed his mother's test and took one.

'Thanks Elsie,' he said as she put it on his plate.

She coloured slightly, smiled at him, took another roll and put it on her own plate. She copied him and broke it open as he had done, spread some butter on and ate heartily.

'What are you up to for the rest of the day Ken?' asked his father.

'Well we cut our walk a bit short this morning,' said Ken. 'I was hoping, if Elsie isn't too tired, to finish it, then go out for a meal somewhere after that.'

'I know you'd be happy walking round there all day,' said Ken's mother, 'but Elsie will have been on her feet long enough and could do with a good sit down this afternoon.'

'I'm used to being on my feet,' said Elsie, finishing off the last of her soup.

'Why, what do you do?'

Without looking, and seeing the triumph flickering on his mother's face, Ken knew Elsie's face was colouring.

'Elsie does cleaning at Temperley's offices,' said Ken, letting his mother know that he was already aware of his girlfriend's background.

'I thought you looked fit,' said Steve Bradshaw, trying to ease Elsie's discomfiture. 'My staff look knackered after being on their feet all day.'

'Thanks for the meal mum,' said Ken. 'Do you mind if we go now?'

'So soon? I've got some ice cream and fruit.'

'That would be lovely,' said Elsie.

Ken's heart warmed even more to her. He knew she was dying to get away but wanted to prove, for his sake, that she wasn't anorexic and wasn't overcome by nerves, even if she was.

They ate the sweet in silence, Ken giving Elsie a comforting smile when she glanced at him.

'I was going to show Elsie the garden,' said Ken's father as they finished and Stella Bradshaw rose to her feet. 'If you've time, that is.'

'I'd love to see it,' said Elsie. 'Can I help with the washing up first though?'

'Ken can help me put it in the dishwasher.'

Ken's father showed Elsie to the back door. 'What do you think of the lungwort?' he asked as they stepped out. 'Not the prettiest of flowers but doing well this year.'

They passed out of earshot as Ken collected the plates from the dining room and carried them into the kitchen.

'You could do better,' his mother said eventually.

'I don't think so.'

97

'She's pretty enough, I'll give you that, but, well.'

'But well what? I'm seeing a girl who attracts me. Yes, partly because she is pretty, but also because we get along well together. We make each other laugh. We interest each other. I don't know, I just like her. I love her in fact.'

His mother sighed.

'She didn't even know what plate to put her roll on, did she? I suppose she doesn't have much call for that sort of thing.'

'What sort of thing?'

'Well, etiquette in general.'

'There is only one golden rule of etiquette mum. That is never ever to embarrass a guest.'

'Even so.'

'Is it because she looks so much like Marion?' Ken asked.

'Of course not.'

'She definitely isn't anorexic.'

'Well she's very thin.'

'I know, but you saw how she tackled her lunch. Once she got the chance she got stuck in and even had a second roll.'

'I know, I know. But your sister was so clever.'

'Of course she was. But not clever enough to see what she was doing to herself.'

'She was ill, Kenneth. She didn't know what she was doing.'

'I'm sorry. But give Elsie a chance, will you?'

'I won't try to stop you. But I've told you already, you could do better.'

Ken shook his head and went out to join Elsie and his father.

'It's lovely Ken,' said Elsie. 'Oh I do wish I had a garden like this.'

'We'll come here again,' said Ken. 'Then perhaps we can sit out here and take it all in. But meanwhile, there are a few more things of Ellen Willmott's to show you, then perhaps we can go to a pub for dinner?'

'You could come back here,' offered Ken's mother, who had followed him out.

'Thanks, but no, I'd like Elsie to myself for a bit,' said Ken firmly.

'Thank-you very much for showing me round Mr Bradshaw,' said Elsie. 'And thank-you for the meal Mrs Bradshaw.'

'Oh, just one thing,' said Ken as they walked back through the house. 'Elsie, do you mind if I just show mum and dad your sketches.'

'Oh no,' she pleaded. 'They're only rough, not very good, I don't show them to people.'

'Please?' said Ken. Then without waiting for an answer he left a reddening Elsie to go to his car.

'I'm sorry,' she said. 'I know what you must be thinking. We probably won't last for long then I'll be out of your lives.'

'No,' protested Ken's father. 'I've not seen Ken happier than over these past few days.'

The front door opened again and Ken brought the sketchpad in. He opened it at the page showing the snowdrop. Ken's father looked at the pencil sketch and gasped.

'Why it's beautiful,' he said, taking the book and going through the pages one by one. 'They are all beautiful. Where did you learn to draw like this Elsie? Did you go to art school?'

'No, I never did. I just like drawing.'

'Have you tried water colours?'

'No, just drawing.'

'You have a real talent.'

'Thank-you.'

She was pleased, but crimson by now.

'Come on then Elsie,' said Ken, taking the pad back.

After getting her seated in the car, he walked quickly back to the door.

'I expect she won't mind giving you a few tips mum,' he whispered.

13

I still wonder at the mystery of Warley Place; the secrets that it holds. Not so much the famous people, Ellen Willmott herself, Jacob Maurer and Robinson. I'd like to know about how the gardeners lived; the ones that had to scratch a living. But we'll never know, will we?

Alfie wearily trudged up the slope, pushing the barrow laden with weeds to the bonfire site. He vowed to himself that he'd never get involved with any dodgy business again. He was stupid to expect anything but trouble, getting mixed up with Wally Barnes. Thank God none of the plants had been touched, otherwise the old bat would have had a field day finding out who had done it. She'd have got to the bottom of it sooner or later, no mistake. He wasn't out of the wood yet though, he knew that. He'd seen the Old Bill talking to her and to Jacob and they'd be back, that was for sure.

Tipping the contents out, Alfie glanced at the coach-house clock. Not long to go, thank God. Perhaps he'd have a quick one at the *Thatchers* before returning home. Bessie wouldn't begrudge him that, would she? Yes, she probably would, but he'd have one anyway. Seeing the police had put the wind up him. Suppose Alfie had told someone where he was going, and more importantly who with? No, he kept his illicit affairs very quiet for very good reason.

He turned to fetch one more load and saw Jacob walking towards him with a man who looked strangely familiar.

'All right Alfie?'

'Yes thanks Jacob.'

'I believe you know Felix Martinsyde?'

Alfie's back straightened as he automatically came to attention.

'Sorry sir, I didn't recognize you in civvies,' he said.

'It's not sir, it's Felix now,' said the ex-lieutenant.

'Mr Martinsyde saved my life,' said Alfie to Jacob. 'He saved all our lives. Fat lot of appreciation he got for it from the brass though, from what I heard.'

'Well, that's in the past now,' said Martinsyde. 'And don't forget you saved my life too, pulling me down like that. Damn fool I was. Sniper would have got me,' he explained to Jacob.

'What are you doing here sir? Oh, sorry, none of my business.'

'No, it's OK. You used to go on so much about Warley Place out there in the trenches that I thought I'd look in while I was in the area. It's everything you said it was and so is Mr Maurer.'

Alfie felt himself redden and noticed Jacob shuffling his feet uncomfortably.

'Do you see anything of your old mates?' asked Martinsyde. 'Ernie Miller? Bert, er, whatsisname?'

'No, we lost contact.'

'What about that other fellow, always scrounging things. Barnes, wasn't it?'

'Wally? Yes, he lives around here somewhere. I see him in the *Thatchers* from time to time. Haven't seen him there lately though.'

'Do you miss those days?'

'In some ways sir. Not the killing of course, and the rats, and the mud. But the comradeship, all in the same boat so to speak, I miss that.'

'I know how you feel.'

'I have not been in that situation,' said Jacob thoughtfully. 'But they say that one can find true contentment if you can reconcile three things. These things are: what you should expect from others; what others should expect from you; and what you expect from yourself. This is difficult whatever path you walk. Perhaps you found it in the Army.'

'Yes, I found that,' said Alfie. 'I could rely on my mates and Mr Martinsyde here, and they could rely on me; we certainly knew what to expect from the Germans and they knew what to expect from us. Until the end, that is. No one expected that. I'll never forget that sir.'

'Well, you'd better be off then Alfie,' said Jacob pulling his watch from his pocket. 'I'll just show Mr Martinsyde round for a bit.'

'I'm glad you're OK sir,' said Alfie, shaking the ex-officer's proffered hand.

'Good to see you Alfie.'

He pushed the barrow to a small shed and made his way down the drive towards the South gate. He was glad the Lieutenant was well, but found himself wondering why he had come to Warley Place. Surely not because of Alfie's comments in the trenches – which in any event had been made to his mates, not to their officer.

Being married had its advantages, but going home to a nagging wife and screaming kids wasn't one of them. He almost envied the unmarried staff who were put up at the bothy. They could have a drink, go back, roll into bed and come back next day with no one to worry about other than themselves.

He glanced at Jacob's little cottage, with its neat garden, by the gate. How on earth did he manage to keep it looking so tidy and do his job as well? And as for having nine children to worry about, and what with his wife being dead too, well it didn't bear thinking about. He liked Jacob. Respected him too.

Ordering his usual, he took it outside and sat himself down on one of the benches, his back to the estate. God it was good to sit down.

He sipped at his beer. Peace at last.

'Well, well, if it ain't Alfie Hedges.'

A sour looking individual came and sat himself down opposite. Alfie's heart sank. It was Bernie, Wally's younger brother. A right nasty piece of work, if ever there was one; little to choose between the two of them, Wally or Bernie. Alfie had been expecting this confrontation eventually and had got his story ready, but now it was happening he suddenly felt frightened. There was no reasoning with these people. The slightest suspicion and he would end up with a knife in his back.

'Bernie.'

Alfie carried on supping his beer.

'So where's Wally then?'

'How should I know? I was supposed to meet him night before last and he never turned up. Left me feeling a right fool.'

Bernie stared at him.

'What's the problem then? He get picked up by the police?'

'He ain't home, that's the problem. And I think you know something about it.'

102

'Listen,' whispered Alfie conspiratorially, leaning forward. 'We was going to do a job together. I was supposed to meet him in Dark Lane. I was there, he wasn't. I expect he found something more to his liking than a few plants.'

'Yeah, he told me that's what he was going to do.'

Thank God I told most of the truth, thought Alfie. When you're lying, always put as much truth in as possible, then you don't get caught out. Not out of the woods yet though.

'That woman didn't catch him, did she? If I thought you'd tipped her off...'

'And what good would that have done me? I needed the money, Wally knew that. The old dragon wouldn't have given me anything for tipping her off, more likely sacked me. And I don't owe her anything. Besides, she was away at the other side of the country.'

Bernie still stared suspiciously at Alfie.

'Well what did happen to him then?'

'I don't know,' said an exasperated Alfie. 'P'raps he bumped into some nasty piece of work on his way to meet me. Put up a fight and got shoved in a ditch somewhere. There's some bad people about at that time of night.'

'You being funny?' snarled Bernie, reaching across the table and grabbing Alfie's shirt.

Alfie, who was somewhat bigger and stronger than Bernie, shoved him away.

'Wally lost me a good night's sleep,' he said. 'All for nothing. It's me that ought to be aggrieved. If you want help looking for him then I'll help. If you don't, then leave me alone.'

'If I find out...' Bernie rose to his feet and waved a finger at Alfie, drawing it across his throat.

'I don't know nothing. If I hear anything I'll let you know,' protested Alfie, feeling his heart beating fast inside his chest.

He supped the rest of his beer down as Bernie left the pub. Best get home.

Trudging down the hill to his little cottage he considered how close he had come to losing what he had, however little that was. He could have been in prison, or he could have ended up with a knife in his belly. Either way he would have lost his family. At least he had a job. The pay was lousy and the hours long, but it

103

just about brought in enough if they were very careful and if he got the occasional rabbit. Willmott didn't mind them doing that, not if Jacob said it was all right. They only ate her crocuses.

Pushing the door of his cottage open he saw his wife sitting by the fireplace, knitting. She made to get up as he entered.

'I'll get your dinner,' she said. 'It's warm in the oven.'

'No,' he said, gently pushing her down. 'You're tired. I'll get it.'

'Gawd, you all right?' she asked, astonished. 'How many beers you had?'

'Only one,' he said.

She sat back down while he got his dinner and brought it in to eat.

'Do anything interesting today?' she asked. He never had, but she always did ask.

'No, the usual. Bernie Barnes came up to me in the pub though. Thought I might know something about Wally going missing.'

'You don't, do you?'

'No, course not.'

'Don't know which one is worse, Wally or Bernie. You keep clear of them.'

'The other night, when I went out poaching.'

'Oh no, you didn't...'

'I was supposed to meet Wally. Willmott hadn't paid me and I was getting desperate. It was supposed to be easy money, but he didn't turn up. I'm glad now, but I was annoyed at the time.'

He didn't like lying to his wife, but knew quite well that someone would come asking and it was better that she believed she was telling the truth.

'And now Wally has gone missing?'

'That's right. The police were round asking questions, but there's no sign that he's been round the gardens. He's been trying to get even with the old girl ever since she showed him up when she and some man caught him trying to steal plants.' He chuckled. 'Wet his pants, apparently. His wife let the cat out of the bag and now everyone knows.'

'So Willmott might have done something to him?'

104

'No, she was away. More likely he got drunk and ended up in a ditch somewhere. Talking of France, my officer, Martinsyde, he came to the garden today.'

'The one that you said was very brave, stopped you all getting killed?'

'Yes, that's the one.'

'What did he want?'

'Dunno,' said Alfie, frowning. 'Said he was in the area and wondered what I was talking about when we was in the trenches.'

He wiped his bread round the plate to soak up the last of the gravy and put it in his mouth.

'That was very nice.'

'Thanks.'

He took his plate out to the kitchen and gave it a quick wipe before coming back in and collapsing into a battered old chair.

'Kids OK?'

'Not bad today. Little Alfie got into a spot of trouble at school, but nothing terrible. He's getting on well with his reading. Margaret is....'

She looked at Alfie. His eyes were closed, his breathing regular. He'd had a hard day. They were mostly hard. He seemed different tonight though. Something had happened to him. He had changed. She hoped it was for the better. It looked like it, but the Barnes brothers worried her. They were a nasty pair and if Alfie was mixed up with them in any way at all then there was trouble ahead. Meanwhile best let him sleep.

Jacob sipped the last of his glass of blackberry wine and read through his letter. They were the pleasures of his evenings, after seeing to the fire and looking in on his children; trying the wine he had made and writing to his sisters in Switzerland. It had been very interesting seeing Alfie's old lieutenant, Martinsyde. Alfie had told him what the officer had done that last time before the cease fire, but hadn't mentioned previously pulling the officer down so that the sniper's bullet just missed him.

He yawned and rubbed his eyes before bending over the paper one last time before signing 'Your affectionate brother, Schaggi', folding it and placing it carefully in an envelope.

14

I was sure you were better off without me after seeing your house and your parents, that's why I decided not to see you again. But I was glad you came for me anyway. My father showed himself up something awful though, I was very embarrassed. I'm frightened what will happen to my mother when I leave home, but leave I must eventually.

'No Elsie again this morning?' asked Peter as they sat down for their tea break. It had been an exhausting morning, pushing the cart full of logs from yet more felled sycamores back to the car park.

'No,' said Ken. 'I went to pick her up but her father said she wouldn't be here this morning.'

'Did she say that too?'

'Well no, I didn't get the chance to speak to her. But if she doesn't want to come I'll just have to accept it.'

'And you're leaving it like that? Ken, anyone can see that she's mad about you. Is she at work this morning?'

'No. At least, I don't think so. She said she was going to re-arrange her work to suit coming here. Except she hasn't come. Like I say, she must have had second thoughts. Mind you, I'm not surprised after meeting my mother.'

'Rubbish. Go round there. Now. If her old man answers the door then insist on seeing her. She's grown-up for goodness sake and so are you. Do you want her?'

'Oh yes.'

'Then go now.'

'Well perhaps after lunch.'

'Now. Why not?'

Ken considered for a moment. If he was honest with himself he was afraid that she had indeed had second thoughts about their relationship and he didn't want to find out for certain. His mother had made it pretty plain that she didn't really think it was a good match. His father had seemed pretty pleased about it at first, but even he had suggested that Ken thought a bit more before letting it get too serious.

'To tell you the truth, I don't want to put too much pressure on her. I wonder if perhaps she is finding it difficult fitting into a group of people she doesn't know and whose ways aren't her ways.'

'Of course she's finding it difficult. Wouldn't you in her position? Do you know what Social Identity is?'

'No idea. But I bet it's something you picked up at your psychology course.'

'Actually you're right,' Peter laughed. 'But it's relevant, so if we could skip the frivolous remarks I'll tell you what little I know. It's all to do with belonging to groups. Your own social identity, your self-esteem, is bound up with how you feel about the groups to which you belong. Elsie feels that the groups to which she belongs – her family, perhaps her work, her circle of friends – are in some way inferior to yours.'

'There's no need for her to think that. I don't bother thinking about whether or not my groups are inferior or superior to others.'

'No, that's because you are content with yours. I've only met her briefly, but I don't think Elsie is happy with hers. So she feels inferior.'

'So if she joins our group that will help?'

'Yes, it will. It's one way of boosting one's self-esteem, but it's a difficult way. If she was rejected by the new group she would be devastated.'

'She wouldn't be rejected by me,' said Ken vehemently.

'No, and not by anyone else here. In fact we would all be delighted if she joined us. And I think she will fit in well on her own account. She shares our values.'

'So what's difficult?'

'The difficult bit may be in reconciling this group with her other groups. She may feel isolated. Her erstwhile friends won't like to see her moving, as they may see it, up to a higher status group. She'll have to be very careful how she plays it.'

'Oh, I see. So if she goes blundering in and tells them how wonderful we all are they will – what, expel her from their group?'

'In effect, they may well do.'

'So I was right. Best leave well alone.'

'No, definitely not. If you are sure about her, which you seem to be, then help her. Otherwise she will spend the rest of her life wondering what might have been. And so will you.'

'I know you're right. So why am I hesitating?'

'Fear of rejection?'

'Ah. Perhaps. Right, I'll go now before you give me a lecture about that too.'

'Good. And don't take no for an answer.'

Ken walked back to the car. That time at school came back to him. He'd really fancied Maureen. She was clever and very pretty and one day he'd plucked up the courage to ask her to come to the pictures. She'd laughed at him. He'd never forgotten the look on her face; the incredulity that someone like her would deign to go out with someone like him. He'd resolved never ever to ask a girl out again. His hormones dictated otherwise, but he'd always had deep-rooted reservations after that and he knew it showed.

But it was different with Elsie. Yes, he would be firm. He wanted her. They felt right together. If she wanted to end it then he would hear it from her own lips, not from her father.

He remembered nothing about the short journey to her house, but as he knocked on the door he found himself more nervous than he could remember. To his relief it was her mother who answered the door.

'Kenneth,' she said, a smile creasing her worn face. 'Elsie has gone to the shops.'

'Oh. I'll come back another time. I just wondered...'

'Would you like to come in and wait?' She fiddled with her apron. 'She won't be long. I'll make a cup of tea. If you want one, that is.'

'That's very kind, I'd like to if I may,' he said.

The poor woman looked pleased he was there but was as nervous as a kitten. Ken wondered what had been going on as she ushered him into the small lounge where her husband was sitting watching the TV.

'Turn that off Henry?' she asked.

Her husband turned round and glared at her, ignoring Ken.

'No, it's all right Mrs Clark, I don't want to disturb Mr Clark. I'm more than happy sitting in the kitchen.'

'I thought I told you she wasn't coming,' Mr Clark said, hardly turning his head from the television.

'You did. But I want to see if she can come out with me again at some other time.'

'She's not coming at all.'

Ken felt his temper rising.

'Then she can tell me that when she returns from the shops.'

He turned to Mrs Clark.

'That cup of tea would be most welcome. The kitchen would be fine.'

He heard a quietly sarcastic 'That cup of tea would be most welcome' from the lounge as he took the few steps to the kitchen.

'I'm sorry about Henry,' she said as she put the kettle on. 'He doesn't really mean to be like that. It's just that not being able to find work – '

'No need to apologise. Life can be very frustrating sometimes and it can bring out the worst in people.'

'Elsie won't be long.'

'May I ask you something Mrs Clark?'

'Of course.'

'I'm very fond of your daughter.' He drew a deep breath. 'Actually I've fallen in love with her. I know I've only known her a very short while, but I'm sure of my feelings. Does she feel the same about me?'

'Please call me Mary. And if you want to know the answer to that question, why not ask her yourself.'

Ken spun round to see Elsie standing there, carrier bag in hand and her mouth wide open, tears in her eyes. He jumped to his feet.

'You know I feel the same way,' she said. 'I've never been happier. But your mother is right. I don't belong in your world. I've had a lovely few days and I'll treasure them, but I'm worried that you will jump into something and regret it later. I thought some time apart might do you good. You can really think about what you want without worrying about letting me down.'

'My mother is frightened of losing me. She's already lost her daughter; I'm all she has left. Marion was very, very bright; a perfectionist in many ways. She could have gone on to great things, but the pressure on her to do so may well have contributed to her anorexia. So please don't take too much notice of what my mother says. Now I've found you I don't want to let you go. I won't let you go, so you might as well give in now. And as for this 'your world' business, my father and mother weren't born with money, they worked very hard for it, both of them. So what do you say?'

'She says yes,' said Mrs Clark.

'I guess I'm outnumbered,' whispered Elsie.

Ken stepped towards her and put his arms round her slender body. She put hers round his own waist, but as he squeezed her he heard her gasp. He let go.

'What is it?'

'Nothing, honestly.'

'And this?' he asked, gently caressing a not very well hidden bruise on her cheek. 'Is it more of that?'

'Please Ken, leave it.'

She was trembling. He looked round at her mother, who was standing frozen with the teapot in her hand.

'All right. For the moment. Fancy coming for a drive then Elsie? We'll give Warley a miss. Let's take a trip to Southend or somewhere and wander along the front. I haven't done that for years.'

'I'd like that.'

'I wouldn't mind that tea though Mrs Clark.'

She smiled and turned to pour it out as Elsie went upstairs to change. Ken quietly left the room and went into the lounge.

'You still here?'

'Just listen. I'll only say it once,' said Ken, his face inches from the other man, his body towering over him. There was rare venom in his voice. 'They won't say how they got them, but any bruises in future on either of those two women and I'll come looking for you. You really don't want to make an enemy out of me, I promise you.'

'Dunno what you're talking about.'

'Really? I think perhaps you'd better work it out then,' said Ken turning away, hoping he hadn't just blown his chances with Elsie and quickly moving back to the kitchen before she came down the stairs.

'Ken,' said Elsie's mother. 'Do you mind if I say something.'

'Oh dear, that sounds ominous. Of course I don't.'

'Elsie thinks the world of you. She's twenty years old and has never had a real steady boyfriend. That's because she takes things so seriously. To be honest I think she's frightened that she might end up like me and her father. I know you can't promise what might happen in the future, but if you aren't as serious as she is then best to call it off now. Sorry, I'm not saying that very well. Like I said before, I'd be so happy if you two stayed together. Just do as she says and think seriously about it, would you?'

'Of course I will. We'll have a talk when we go out today, but I don't have any doubts whatsoever.'

'What about your parents?'

'I am twenty-three, so it doesn't really matter what they think. But actually my father has really taken to her and I think my mother will too.'

They both fell silent as Elsie reappeared. Ken gulped down the last of his tea and got to his feet.

'Thanks for the chat,' he said. 'We'll have something to eat while we are out.'

'See you later then,' she replied.

'Goodbye Mr Clark,' Ken said as he passed the lounge door.

'Goodbye dad.'

They smiled at a grunted reply, but at least it was a response.

'I'm happy to go to Southend,' said Ken as they settled themselves into his car. 'But have you been to Thorndon?'

'I went to an art exhibition once, but that's all. I went for a short walk but got a bit lost. I've been to Southend with the girls at work so Thorndon would be great.'

'Actually I'm not dressed for walking round Southend,' said Ken. 'Although if anyone sees you at Thorndon they'll wonder who the scruffy bloke is.'

'There are so many different places I want you to see,' he continued as they left the houses behind and drove down the tree-lined road to Thorndon country park.

'I can't wait for you to take me.'

He turned into the car park and eased his car into a space near a ticket machine.

'We'll pop in there later and have a drink and a snack,' he said nodding towards the big visitor centre. 'I should warn you that I sometimes get lost here though,' he continued, grinning as he locked the car. 'I've got a trail guide but it's at home.'

'Let's just walk and see where we get to,' said Elsie as she took his hand.

They headed off, bypassing the visitor centre, following the wide path into the trees.

'Things seem to be moving rather fast,' she said eventually as they stopped to look at a particularly old oak tree.

'Too fast?'

'Not for me. But I'm worried about you.'

'I've only known you for just over a week,' he said. 'But I meant what I said to your mother. I do love you. It's strange how two people can meet and know immediately that they are right for each other. Do you think that applies to us?'

'I knew we were as soon as you came up to me by the pond at Warley Place,' she said. 'But don't say anything about that to your parents yet, will you? They might see things differently. I think your mum is just waiting for it to all blow over.'

'All right,' said Ken. 'I'll leave it until tomorrow.'

'Ken!'

'No, seriously, I know what you mean. They don't have to know yet. Although I think perhaps they already do.'

He hesitated and then spoke.

'There's something you should know.'

'You've already got a wife and three children?'

'No, seriously. Remember that blonde man who you thought was following you at Warley Place.'

'Oh, him. Yes. There was something about him I didn't like.'

'He used to work for us. For my father, I mean, in one of our garden centres. We had to get rid of him. He wasn't following you, he was following me.'

'He's not gay, is he?'

'No, it's not that. He was stealing from us. Just little things at first, but it got too much.'

'And he didn't like it. Funny how people always think it isn't fair when they get caught.'

'No, it's more than that Elsie. His family has been in the area for donkey's years, the same as mine. The story had been passed down that there was some stealing going on at Warley Place in

Ellen Willmott's time, which is when our nursery was really started. Only a stall at the market to begin with, but my great grandfather worked hard, eventually bought some land and it grew from there.'

'And he says that it was started on the proceeds of stolen goods?'

'Exactly. He told my father that if he didn't get his job back he'd tell everyone. My dad told him that it wasn't true and if he did spread that story then dad would have him for slander.'

'So what's the problem?'

'Well I think he's angry enough to do it anyway. It's one of those things that's difficult to disprove and reputation is everything in business. But meanwhile he's trying to put pressure on me to get dad to take him back.'

'You're not going to, are you?'

'No fear. What worries me though is that now he's seen me with you he might try a different approach. He'll intimidate you. It's no secret that he's on drugs and he's pretty unstable when he hasn't had his fix. I'm frightened he might get rough with you to get money out of me.'

'No he won't. He might try it, but he won't succeed. There's no truth in the story, is there? Not that it would matter if there was.'

'I really don't know,' said Ken. 'I know that after Ellen Willmott died a lot of the plants were taken by the legitimate heirs to Spetchley Park and planted there, which was good. But much of what was left was in fact stolen and sold locally. I'm pretty sure my great grandfather wasn't involved either then or before, but who knows what can happen when people are desperate.'

'So if he does spread the story round that your business was founded on stolen plants, would it affect trade very much?'

'It probably would if the newspapers got hold of it, which they would,' said Ken. 'But even more important to my father is his good name.'

'But there's no question about him doing anything illegal, is there?'

'No, not at all, but Barnes will make the most of it and the press will want a good story. It could all get very unpleasant.'

They wandered along in silence for a while, hand in hand, identifying some of the trees and wild flowers, wondering about the others.

'Ah, at least I know where we are now,' said Ken as a large lake appeared through the trees. 'That's Childerditch pond. It used to be used by monks to rear fish. Carp, I think.'

They walked slowly round the water, looking at the ducks, until they came to a path leading through open grassland away and back towards the visitor centre.

'This isn't the path we came along, is it?' queried Elsie.

'No, it's a sort of circular route. This is a more interesting way.'

'Oh good. Interesting how?'

'Interesting in that the last three times I've done it I've got lost.'

Elsie giggled.

'However,' he continued, 'we are in luck today. The sun is out and the visitor centre is north-west of here. So since it's nearly midday if we keep the sun behind us and slightly to the right we'll be going in the right direction.'

'That sounds simple enough.'

'It is. The trouble is the paths don't generally run in quite that direction!'

'Any chance of getting lost enough to have to spend the night here?' Elsie asked hopefully, her arm now round his waist and his round hers.

'I think my mother will have the search party out if I haven't reported back by tea time,' he laughed.

They eventually saw the woods in the distance and making for them they were once again amongst trees, with paths seemingly leading in all directions. For once his sense of direction did not fail him and they glimpsed the visitor centre in the distance.

'Thanks for a lovely walk,' Elsie said. 'Are we going back to your house?'

'No fear,' Ken replied. 'We'll have a drink and a snack here, then think about what to do next. I'll ring my mother to let her know. Are you working this afternoon?'

'No,' she said, frowning 'just this evening. I think I've blown the day jobs, my agent wasn't at all pleased.'

'You're worried about it? I'll have a word with dad, he'll soon find something if you want it.'

'It's OK, I'll be fine. It's just that I don't like letting people down. They've had to find someone at short notice. It's not fair on them.'

He nodded and led her into the building.

'Have a look round,' he suggested, waving at the shelves loaded with all sorts of things from clothing, books and binoculars to pencils and cards. 'I'll get us some tea and cakes.'

She felt a little self-conscious on her own so soon moved into the eating area and found a table near a window.

'Ken, it will be all right, won't it?' she asked anxiously a little later as she sipped her tea.

'What do you mean?'

'You know, you and me.'

He put his hand over hers.

'It'll be fine,' he promised.

15

I bet Ellen Willmott liked showing off her garden. I would. It must have been brilliant, pointing out trees and plants that her visitors had probably never even heard of, got from all over the world. A bit like you did for me, that first time we met.

Alfie straightened from his weeding and rubbed his aching back as Jacob spoke, pointing to a small plant nestling in the rocks, covered in small pink flowers.

'And that one?'

'*Dianthus gracilis*,' he said slightly tentatively. 'From Yugoslavia I believe.'

'Very good,' came a voice from behind them.

'Sorry Miss Willmott,' said Jacob Maurer. 'We were working, but I like to teach what little I know to those who are keen to learn. It does not affect – '

'It's all right Jacob,' she said. 'I know you do it, and I like to encourage those who wish to know more.'

She turned to Alfie.

'But do you know it because it is here in this place, or could you recognize it elsewhere?'

'I think it is a little of both madam,' said Alfie nervously. 'I have little doubt that you could produce another example which to my untrained eye would look the same but which would be named differently.'

'A good answer. And what is that?'

She pointed at a small clump comprising glossy leaves and deep blue flowers on very short stems, the whole being no more than three or four inches high.

'*Gentiana acaulis*, otherwise known as Stemless gentian.'

'Not *Gentiana verna* then?'

'No madam. The flowers are more trumpet shaped and have green-spotted throats. Also *Gentiana verna* has mostly lost its flowers by now, as this soon will.'

'Very good.'

She consulted her watch.

'Some members of the Essex Field Club will be arriving shortly. They will be walking up from the station and will arrive at approximately half past two. Robinson will give them a drink at the conservatory, then at three o'clock I should like you to show them round.'

'Yes Miss Willmott,' said Jacob.

'No, not you Jacob, I think we may let Alfie take them.'

'But I know so little. What if they ask – '

'They will not ask. They are very knowledgeable. If they do and you are uncertain as to the answer then when you meet Jacob at the gorge you can ask him, or failing that I can answer questions at the end. There is one thing to watch, which may require some tact but also firmness.'

Alfie saw a smile cross Jacob's face.

'One or two of them may have small trowels or scissors and big pockets,' she said.

'Oh I am sure not,' said Alfie, before cringing at the icy stare he received.

'You will get cleaned up before they arrive, but will wear your working clothes so that you may continue with your work as soon as they leave.'

She made to walk off and then turned back to Alfie.

'What do you know about a thief who tried to steal my plants and is now missing?' she asked, her unblinking eyes fixed on his.

Alfie felt his face redden. She knew. Who had told her? Not Jacob, surely?

Jacob turned to her and whispered something in her ear. As they stepped away out of earshot Alfie's heart sank. He would be sacked, he knew that, but would she inform the police? Damn Wally Barnes to hell. He hoped that's where he had gone.

He saw Ellen Willmott turn and look at him. What could he say to her? Nothing, that's what. She would certainly not be swayed by anything he could say in his defence. After all, he had been helping someone to steal her plants. Oh well, he thought as they turned and came back towards him, just take it and go.

'I think there is a little more to it than Mr Maurer is willing to say,' she said. 'But the fact remains that you saved his life. A villain is missing and I am not concerned with his whereabouts as long as he stays missing. I understand he is the same nasty piece of work who tried to rob me once before and while I am not afraid of meeting him again I am glad I will probably never need to do so. I wish to hear no more of the matter.'

She turned to leave, then turned back again.

'It is sometimes the way of the Essex Field Club to pass a small appreciation to those showing them round,' she said. 'If that is the case today, you may keep it.'

She strode off.

'Well,' said Jacob. 'It is usual that either she or Robinson take anything in the way of tips. You are privileged.'

'And very much appreciated it will be. But what did you tell her?' asked Alfie.

'No more than she needed or wanted to know,' said Jacob. 'She no doubt guesses the rest, but knows where your loyalties lie. Just do your best and no more will be heard of the matter. Just concentrate on showing your visitors round this afternoon.'

'Oh, yes, I'd forgotten about them. But what do I say to them?'

'Just explain what the various areas are for, and tell them about some of the plants. You know them as well as anyone and if you talk about the ones you do know they won't have time to ask about those you don't.'

'What if they do try to pinch any?'

Jacob laughed.

'They won't do that. You know how paranoid she gets about people stealing from her. These people wouldn't dream of taking advantage in such a way.'

'I hope not,' sighed Alfie. 'I can't imagine getting one of the old dears in an arm lock and marching her back to the main house!'

'Now that would be a sight to see,' chuckled Jacob. 'Go on lad, go and get cleaned up, you don't want to be late. Use my cottage, Friedi will let you in, she knows you well enough.'

'Thanks Mr Maurer,' said Alfie. 'And thanks for sorting things out about, well, you know what.'

'That's all right,' said Jacob, looking warily about. 'But please don't mention it again. Not ever. You never know when she might have crept up behind you and if she hears the rest of the story you definitely will get the sack.'

Alfie hurried down the hill to the South Lodge. Things did seem to be picking up a bit. He loved learning about the plants and would like to grow some of his own, but working twelve hours a day for five days a week and ten on Saturday meant that he didn't get much time to do anything else, let alone yet more gardening.

Fifteen minutes later, hands clean, face washed, hair more or less in place and his apron and hat straightened, he walked nervously to the conservatory.

His jaw dropped and his knees went weak when he saw them. They were being addressed by Ellen Willmott.

There were at least a dozen of them there. One was a little chap with white hair, red nose, a waxed moustache, a stick and a superior expression on his face. He seemed to be vying for leadership of the group with a thin-faced woman, her hair done up inside a huge wide-brimmed hat and a pair of ridiculous boots designed to show that she was a country woman rather than from the town but proving the opposite.

Of the others, one earnest-looking woman was staring intently at their host, jotting something down in her little notebook from time to time. Apart from one young couple who seemed more interested in each other than the garden, the rest were a mixture of old and young, male and female, but they all had something in common: they looked horribly knowledgeable.

'Ah, Alfie,' Ellen Willmott said as he approached. 'Very timely. These good people wish to look round the garden so perhaps you could escort them?'

The moustached gentleman looked Alfie up and down.

'Does this chap know the names of the plants,' he asked.

'Major, I have approaching one hundred thousand different plants here,' said Ellen Willmott imperiously. 'Even I would have to refer to my records to determine the names of some of them. So no, Alfie will not know all of them; in fact he will not know most of them. But he will be able to identify more than you will be able to remember when you leave here.'

Several of the group smiled and nodded in friendly fashion at Alfie. The young couple giggled at each other. The elderly woman looked smug.

'Right, if there are no other questions I will leave you in Alfie's capable hands.'

Without waiting to hear if there were in fact any more questions she turned on her heel and moved away from the group.

'Right,' said Alfie as confidently as he could manage but unable to stop his voice from shaking a little. He wanted to be on familiar ground before going very far with this lot. 'If you could follow me we will perhaps first look at what many believe to be the best Alpine garden in Europe.'

'I suggest we see go to the old orchard area first to look at the rockery, then down past the boating lake,' said the major, testing Alfie's leadership qualities no doubt.

'No, we'll go to the walled garden first, then to the orchard area,' said the elderly lady.

'Mrs Fitzwalter, Major,' said the woman with the notebook. 'May I suggest that since Alfie knows the gardens better than we do, then we let him lead us where he may.'

'He may well know the gardens better than we do Mrs Harris,' said Mrs Fitzwalter, 'but he doesn't know what our likes and dislikes are.'

'We all have different likes and dislikes,' said Mrs Harris as firmly as she could manage. 'We would all end up going in different directions. No, we must do what Alfie has suggested. Lead on Alfie.'

'The reason I suggested the alpine garden first,' said Alfie, 'is that it may be tiring and if we then go to the walled garden we may feel the need to sit a while before continuing to the old orchard area and rockery.'

'Nonsense,' retorted the major. 'Do you think we're past it then? Let me tell you we've walked – '

'No, I wasn't thinking of you major. But if you are still full of energy when we return then while some of us may be sitting admiring the overview you may walk round the walled garden as many times as you wish.'

'Don't be impertinent man.'

The group had their backs to the house and it was only Alfie who saw, to his horror, the face of Ellen Willmott appear. To his amazement he saw her smile to herself before she continued her walk back to the house.

'If you'll follow me then,' said Alfie, 'we will walk along the outside of the south wall of the walled garden...'

'Would have been easier to go in there first,' grumbled Mrs Fitzwalter.

'... to the Evelyn's chestnuts...'

The young man whispered something about Evelyn's chestnuts to his girlfriend who started to giggle.

'... and then to the alpine garden.'

As Alfie led them along the wall he heard the words he had been dreading.

'What's that then?' one of the group asked, pointing at a plant growing out of a gap between two bricks. It looked like an ivy but had small leaves and little light blue flowers. Alfie breathed a sigh of relief.

'That's an Ivy-leaved toadflax,' he said. '*Cymbalaria muralis.* It is native in Italy. First recorded in Britain near here at Stubbers about three hundred years ago.'

'Good grief, I thought everyone knew that,' muttered the major loudly.

The questioner did not look the least bit surprised or put out by the major's comment so Alfie assumed that they were all used to his attitude. He waited while Mrs Harris scribbled in her notebook and found himself looking to see if any of the group had large pockets. Then, suddenly thinking that they may well have known what was going through his mind, he felt his face heating and turned to lead on.

Stopping briefly to look at an example of *Umbellaria californica,* the well-known headache tree that was reputed to bring about a headache if one was unwise enough to sniff at a leaf when crushed, they stood in front of the Spanish chestnuts.

'Planted by John Evelyn, don't y'know?' commented the major.

'Well, there is some doubt about that,' said Alfie. 'That very large-boled one probably was, but the others are thought by some to be just a little too young.'

'Stuff and nonsense.'

'Why, were you there when they were planted?' said Mrs Fitzwalter.

'He's old enough,' laughed one of the group, who took care not to show his face.

'Magnificent trees, anyway,' said Mrs Harris, scribbling again.

'Aren't they lovely,' said someone, pointing to the delicate narcissi covering the grass in front of the big trees.

'Yes, they are, aren't they,' said Alfie. '*Narcissus triandrus*.'

'We knew that,' said the major.

'They are rather late this year,' continued Alfie. 'They have usually gone by now.'

'Lovely view of London from here,' said the major as they looked out over the west meadow. 'Second highest place in Essex, this.'

'In my opinion no view of London is lovely,' said Mrs Fitzwalter. 'But then I always do prefer the country.'

The major looked pityingly at her.

Mrs Harris scribbled again. Alfie wondered briefly if she was keeping the score.

They moved on.

'Where's Millie?' said someone.

'And Charlie?'

The two of them appeared from behind one of the chestnuts, walking fast to catch up with the group, Millie straightening her dress.

'Lovely view,' said Charlie.

Millie convulsed in giggles again.

'The Persian ironwood tree,' said Alfie, pointing to his left. '*Parrotia persica*.'

'It's a bit of a mess, isn't it?' said the major. 'Needs pruning, in my opinion. Branches going in all sorts of directions.'

'Rubbish,' said Mrs Fitzwalter rather predictably. 'Part of its charm is the way the branches go. Look, that one bends right back on itself. Prune it and it'll look just like any other tree.'

'What do you think Mr.... er.... Alfie?' asked Mrs Harris.

'We do like to let our trees develop in a way that is natural to them,' Alfie said, 'rather than in the way that might be more pleasing to our own eye. If you look closely you will see how the branches fuse together when they meet, resulting in what many see as an interesting pattern.'

The major snorted.

'It is fairly recent in this country,' said Alfie. 'Discovered by a Mr Parrott, hence its name. As a specimen tree it was planted to mark the beginning of the alpine garden.'

Indeed, large boulders could now be seen, and the beginnings of a deep gorge.

They moved on to the bridge over the gorge. Even those who had seen it before, which included the major and Mrs Fitzwalter, were moved to silence as they gazed upon this incredible work of art.

'Would you like me to take over for this part of the tour?' asked Jacob, climbing up from the stream at the bottom.

'I could do with a break,' admitted Alfie. Then to the group, 'This is Mr Jacob Maurer, who Mrs Willmott brought all the way from Switzerland to develop and manage her alpine garden. He is a renowned expert in the field and will take over for this part of the tour.'

Alfie sat on a large rock, one with *Primula sikkimensis* planted by it, and listened while Jacob stunned even the major with his knowledge of the plants. He often sat on this particular rock. There was a strange peace emanating from it. He'd said so once to Jacob, who had nodded in agreement but would not say anything further. He had been scared stiff of showing these people round, but found he was actually enjoying himself and looked forward to continuing the tour.

One of the group was a bit of a fern expert and wanted to look in the filmy fern cave, built to house ferns that would otherwise not have survived, but Jacob suggested that rather than hold the whole group up she might like to come on her own at some stage, when he would be glad to show her its contents.

After approximately one half of an hour Alfie was continuing with the tour, down the hill to the main drive and then back to the conservatory. Even the major was puffing a bit by the time they reached the walled garden.

'Right,' said Alfie. 'Some of us will sit here for a while and rest our weary legs. I will arrange for some drinks.'

'And you can trot round the garden to show how fit you are,' said Mrs Fitzwalter to the major, who ignored her and sat down on one of the benches by the south-east corner of the garden.

123

Almost immediately the tall figure of the butler Robinson appeared, pushing a trolley laden with glasses and jugs of lemonade.

While they were all quenching their thirst and resting their legs Alfie pointed out the main trees in this part of the garden: the several magnolias, the Chusan palm and the magnificent Ginkgo biloba.

Walking slowly round the flat paths of the walled garden was found to be much easier than the walk to the alpine garden and the area covered was considerably less, but the number of flowers and other plants to be seen demanded frequent stops for admiration, particularly of the more unusual species.

Finally Alfie had to admit defeat when the major pointed out an anemone with pretty bluish flowers and asked what variety it was. One of the group suggested that it might be *Anemone hepatica*, which Ellen Willmott later confirmed was the case.

As they walked back out of the garden Alfie noticed Mrs Harris glancing anxiously at her watch.

'I say everybody,' she said.

Nobody took the least bit of notice.

'Halt,' said the major in a tone that commanded immediate response. 'Mrs Harris has something to say and I have a feeling I know what it is.'

'Thank-you major. We are rapidly running out of time to catch our train,' she said. 'We have to thank our hostess and to reach the station before it leaves.'

There were murmurs from those assembled, suddenly silenced as Ellen Willmott appeared.

'We are most disappointed, Miss Willmott, at having to leave before our planned itinerary is completed,' said Mrs Harris. 'However I think I speak for everyone when I say that, er, Alfie has done an excellent job and has a remarkable grasp of the garden.'

'Hear hear,' several of those waiting intoned.

'Well I would be delighted to welcome you on a future occasion during which you may see the remainder of the garden,' said Ellen Willmott.

'You are most gracious,' said Mrs Harris, starting to curtsey but thinking better of it. 'I think Major Williams would like to propose a vote of thanks.'

'Yes, indeed,' coughed the major. 'May I pass on our hearty thanks to you for your kind hospitality, and say that I for one look forward very much to another visit. There is so much to see here it would not be possible to take it all in during just one visit, nay not two or even three.'

'You are most kind,' said Ellen Willmott and the group broke up to go to the station.

Alfie stood there, suddenly feeling lonely and exposed. What would Miss Willmott say now she knew he had taken too long? And Mrs Harris, Mrs Fitzwalter and the major were all having a word with her. He was for it now. He turned to go back to his work.

'Wait there a moment Alfie,' came that strident call he knew so well.

The major, having said his goodbyes to Ellen Willmott, came striding over.

'Well done young fella,' he said, holding out his hand.

Alfie, somewhat amazed, took the proffered hand and found a shilling in his palm.

'No, there's no need,' he protested.

'Keep it, there's a good lad,' said the major. 'You did a good job. Should be rewarded, what?'

'Well, thank-you,' said Alfie.

As the major strode off to join those who had just left, Mrs Harris came up to him.

'Several of us thought we should like to reward good service,' she said. 'You are a talented guide.'

'No, really, there is no need,' protested an embarrassed Alfie. 'The major has already done so.'

'Ah yes, the major does like to do his own thing. Well here is some more.'

She pressed no less than five shillings into his hand.

'You are so very kind,' he said, overcome at their generosity. 'I shall take my good wife out for a meal tonight.'

'You are welcome,' she said. 'I am sorry to have to dash now. Good day to you.'

'Good day. Safe journey,' he said.

'Alfie,' he heard. 'Come here.'

That was the good bit over, he thought. Now for the down side.

'I have heard good reports of you today,' Ellen Willmott said. 'Not an easy lot to deal with, are they?'

'They were most interested in your garden madam,' Alfie said.

'You have a talent that has escaped my attention up to now,' she said. 'We must see what can be done with it. You may go home now.'

'Thank-you madam,' he said. Very good of her, he thought to himself as he turned to go, considering it was already half an hour after his finishing time.

16

That accident with the tree was nasty, wasn't it? I tried not to be frightened, but I was. I wish they hadn't made all that fuss though. Everyone was thanking me, but it was me who should have been thanking them. It made me feel really good, doing something worthwhile. Most people never get the chance to do anything like that.

Ken pulled up outside Elsie's door. He was glad she didn't feel that she needed to dash out to meet him now, to avoid him seeing her home or her parents. He walked up the short path and knocked on the door.

'Hello Elsie,' he beamed as she opened it, leaning forward to kiss her on the lips.

'I won't be a second,' she said. 'I've got everything packed.'

'Hi Mrs Clark, hi Mr Clark,' he called.

Mrs Clark came bustling out.

'Hello Ken.' Then as Elsie came past with her rucksack and boots, 'Have a nice day, both of you.'

'Aye, have a nice day,' echoed a voice from the lounge.

'Thanks,' he answered, watching Elsie's eyebrows rise at sound of her father's voice.

Elsie carefully placed her rucksack in the back of the car, along with her new boots. Ken had insisted on buying her everything she needed for working on the reserve. When she had tried to stop him, he said it was for safety's sake and he'd buy the boots anyway even if they were the wrong size. In the end she gave in and let him. The boots, the gloves, the rucksack, a set of strong waterproofs – he said her dainty ones just weren't suitable for pulling up brambles in – and even some pads for her knees for when she was kneeling. She had her own jeans and an old sweat shirt, and a sandwich box which he assumed was full of food and a drink.

'I'm really looking forward to today,' she said.

'Me too.'

'What did you say to dad?'

'Why do you think I said anything?'

'Because he hasn't been that well behaved for a long time.'

'Perhaps he's looking forward to getting rid of you,' Ken laughed.

'You're not answering the question.'

'I let him know I'd noticed the bruises, and suggested that it wouldn't happen again. Something like that.'

Elsie was silent, apparently having decided not to probe any more. He was relieved that it had worked – for the moment, anyway.

Ten minutes later they were pulling up in the car park.

Daphne came up, smiling and holding her clipboard.

'Lovely to see you again Elsie.'

'I'm looking forward to some hard work,' she said.

An older man, fit-looking with black hair, a greying beard and a twinkle in his eye came up.

'Hi, good to see you again Elsie. And you of course Ken, but mostly Elsie.' Then in a loud aside to Elsie, 'Perhaps we'll get some work out of him now you're back.'

'You met Gordon last time, didn't you?' said Ken, rolling his eyes at the comment. 'Oh, and this is Donald.'

'Just don't take any notice of what that man says,' said Donald pointing at Gordon. 'He almost got one new volunteer to polish the holly leaves on one bush because they weren't as shiny as those on the one next to them! If he says what nice weather it is, just check to make sure.'

'You are hurtful,' said Gordon plaintively. 'Anyway, I'm looking after Elsie today.'

'I don't think so,' said Ben, coming over with a piece of paper covered in scribbles. Ben was the assistant warden and usually responsible for allocating duties for the day.

'Hello Elsie. I wasn't sure if you were coming so I haven't got you down for anything in particular, which means you can take your choice. And since Gordon is going to be fetching logs from the orchard area I'd recommend you give him a miss.'

'Has anyone told you how mean you can be?' asked Gordon with a hurt look on his face.

'I'm bagging leaf mould here,' said Donald. 'She could do that if she wants. I'll do the lifting, but we can take it in turns sieving it. Unless you'd rather stick with Ken, Elsie?'

'I'd like to get to know everyone,' said Elsie, 'so it's probably best if I have a go at the leaf mould.'

'Get to know some of this lot and you probably won't come any more,' said Ben. 'Donald's harmless enough though, so leaf mould it is.'

'Anyway, you're pushing the cart with me,' said Gordon, grinning at Ken, who groaned. 'Peter and Martin are already up there. At least it's mostly downhill and you'll be able to check up on Elsie each time we dump the logs.'

'I don't need to check up on her!' Ken protested.

Gordon just laughed.

'The wind's getting up a bit,' said Ken.

'She'll be all right.'

'I know, I know.'

'You really are serious about her, aren't you?' said Gordon as they started to walk up the drive to collect the trolley and load it with logs. Ken turned and saw Donald explaining the leaf mould procedure to Elsie. She looked up and waved. He waved back.

'Yes, I am,' he said.

'And she's serious about you?'

'Yes, she is.'

'Then make the most of it. Don't waste the best years of your life. Well, actually I'm quite enjoying my current years too, but you know what I mean.'

They glanced at the walnut tree as they passed the turning circle.

'Ben wants us to get the loose concrete off and re-do the top part,' Gordon said. 'Probably next week.'

'I can't believe its still standing,' said Ken. 'If it needed concrete to support it all those years ago, presumably in the late twenties, then it should have fallen over long before now.'

By the time they reached the cart Peter and Martin had half-filled it with split logs. David was wielding one axe and as they loaded the cart Ben appeared and picked up another.

'Oh God,' groaned Gordon, picking up a couple of logs and stacking them on the cart. 'We'll be doing this all day. Isn't it tea break yet?'

'Stop moaning,' grinned Ben. 'Oh, and when you are down there could you bring another pair of loppers back with you?'

'Oh, all right,' grumbled Gordon.

'I think that's enough,' said Martin after a few more minutes of stacking.

'I hear you were causing trouble again last weekend,' said Peter.

'Me?' said Gordon indignantly.

'Yes, you. Something about treading on daffodils? Telling visitors you were a visitor too and that you were made to cart logs about because you accidentally trod on a daffodil?'

'Ah, yes, well it was Ben's fault too, he told me to stop moaning and get on with it.'

'Good God,' said Martin. 'They didn't believe you, did they?'

'Well, for a few seconds,' admitted Gordon.

'What with that and the purple toothwort.'

'There's more?'

'No, that was me being genuinely helpful,' explained Gordon.

'Funny that,' said Peter. 'You're the only one who can get people into trouble by being genuinely helpful.'

'I saw this couple who seemed really interested in the flowers,' explained Gordon. 'So I told them where to find the purple toothwort. When they came back they told me they had been got by the Gestapo. They'd strayed off the path to get a closer look and been spotted by a volunteer who explained that they shouldn't really go off the path. They weren't really annoyed; he told them it was for their own safety as well as to make sure plants didn't get trodden on. They were just a bit embarrassed at being caught.'

'But basically it was your fault,' suggested Peter.

'Er. I'll have to think about that.'

After chasing the cart down the slope, then bouncing it over the drainage channels, they heaved it round the corner to the car park. Elsie looked up from behind the pallets of logs where she was shovelling leaf mould through a mesh balanced on top of a wheelbarrow.

'Come on,' Ken heard Donald say. 'Let's have a break and watch that lot work for a change.'

As the two of them came out from behind the pallets Ken's heart warmed at the sight of Elsie's now dirty face wreathed in a contented smile.

'Not too much for you?' he asked as she approached.

'Are you kidding?' Donald interjected, as Elsie shook her head. 'She's working me into the ground.'

Peter looked up anxiously as they heard a creaking noise from the large sycamore alongside the hut they used as a store.

'The wind's getting up a bit,' he commented.

'It's been a lot worse than this though,' said Donald.

'I don't like it,' said Ken. 'If that comes down it – RUN!'

He grabbed Elsie and they ran back towards the cars, Donald following them, as with an ear-splitting crash a huge section tore itself free from the trunk and smashed down on top of the hut, demolishing both it and the leaf-mould kit behind the pallets. Ken felt sick at the thought of what might have happened to Elsie and Donald had he, Gordon and the others been a few minutes later arriving, or the other two had carried on working.

'That was a near one,' gasped Martin. 'Hey, where's Gordon.'

But Peter was already running to the hut.

'He went inside to get the loppers,' he shouted. 'Someone dial 999, quickly.'

Ken whipped his phone out.

'Damn, no signal,' he said. 'Anyone else got – '

'Try 112,' said Martin, running to join Peter.

To his amazement Ken was soon connected to the emergency services and telling them how to get there.

'Gordon,' Peter was shouting. 'Can you hear me?'

The hut was matchwood, the mangled roof now only a metre from the ground and the walls and door non-existent, the whole covered by a jumble of leaves, twigs and branches surrounding the thick trunk itself. The chance of finding anyone alive in there was so remote as to be negligible.

'My God!' gasped a voice behind them.

Ken turned to see a couple of visitors who had just completed their walk. 'Is there anything we can do?'

'One of you could go back up the path and tell the people that are working there, and get them to bring tools with them. We can at least start to get the branch off.'

'I'll do that,' said the woman, turning and running back the way they had just come.

'Careful,' said Peter as Martin started to pull at the broken pieces of wood. 'If he is alive it could all come down on him.'

Ken ran to his car, grabbed a torch and returned.

'Quiet for a moment,' said Martin before calling 'Can you hear us Gordon?'

There was just silence.

'Look, there's a space at the bottom,' Ken said, kneeling down and shining his torch into it. The branches must be holding the trunk off the ground slightly. Christ, what a mess. Wait, I can see him. Part of him, anyway. He's lying alongside the bench. It's the bench that's taking most of the weight. If that goes he doesn't stand a chance.'

Ken turned to Elsie, standing there shaking and as white as a sheet.

'Go and sit in the car,' he suggested.

'No, I'm all right.'

'Can we get in?' asked Martin.

'No chance,' said Peter. 'The hole is too small. If we disturb anything we could bring the lot down then there will be two casualties instead of one.'

'But he might need help. He could be alive.'

Ken didn't say anything. They were clutching at straws.

Suddenly Elsie was bending down at the hole.

'Can I have the torch?' she asked.

Ken passed it to her.

'I can get in there. I'm half the size of any of you.'

'No,' said Ken. 'Leave it to the emergency services.'

'You've already said he might need help. He's certainly unconscious. If he comes to he may not know where he is and thrash around. Then it could all cave in.'

'No,' repeated Ken firmly, but Elsie already had her head and shoulders in the hole.

'Oh God, no!' he groaned, frightened to grab her in case she wriggled, with the result he most feared.

'She's got guts, I'll say that,' said Martin. 'It's too late to stop her, so let's help.'

'For God's sake be careful Elsie,' cried Ken as her feet disappeared into the hole. 'Take it very slowly and don't move anything.'

It took several very nerve-wracking minutes before they heard her voice.

'He's all right,' she called. 'He's got a bad cut on his head and he was unconscious, but he's just coming round now.'

They heard a muffled conversation as she reassured him.

'Can he feel his arms and legs?' asked Peter.

'He can feel them and move them,' she said, 'but it looks very precarious in here. I think we need to get him out.'

'We can't move him,' said Peter. 'If we do and he's hurt his back or broken a bone we could make things worse.'

There was a creaking sound.

'For Christ's sake come out, Elsie,' begged Ken.

'I can't just leave him.'

'He can't wriggle out any more than we could wriggle in,' said Peter.

'What about a rope round his ankles?' suggested Ken. 'Like pulling a calf out when it's born. It must be better than leaving him there.'

'It could bring the lot down. And as I said, if he's broken anything serious it could make it worse.'

There was a groaning noise as the mass of wood settled further.

'It's a gamble, either way,' said Martin. 'If we leave him, it may all cave in before the fire and rescue people get here and will they do any better anyway? If we try to pull him out the same thing might happen.'

'Elsie, we're going to pass a rope in,' called Ken. Tie it round his ankles, then come out. We'll pull him out when you are safe.'

'Right,' said Elsie. 'But he's still very confused. You'll have to get him out first. I'll come out after him and guide his head.'

'Elsie, please,' begged Ken as Peter threw the end of the rope into the shed.

A few minutes later, just as Frank and Ben came running up, Elsie called out for them to pull.

'Oh God, please let her be all right,' begged Ken. 'Let both of them be all right.'

They very slowly started to pull.

'Hold it,' called Elsie once as his arms got caught, but soon his legs, then his body and finally his head appeared and they

133

carefully but speedily pulled him away from the hut. Close behind emerged a very dirty but triumphant Elsie. Ken bent down and pulled her clear, then as they staggered away from the wreckage there was a final screech of tortured wood as the bench collapsed under the strain and a cloud of dust rose into the air.

Ken grabbed Elsie and wrapped his arms round her, unable to say anything, his eyes filling with tears.

Peter was trying to get Gordon to lay still on an old blanket he'd got from his car as the sound of sirens told them help was approaching, and a minute later first an ambulance and then a fire engine came lurching into the car park.

'Thanks Elsie,' Gordon said as he eventually gave up trying to get to his feet.

'You'd have done it for me.'

'Did you get the loppers out?' he grinned, making one last effort to sit up before his eyes glazed over and he collapsed back on the blanket.

They moved aside as two ambulance men walked quickly up with their bags.

'Who's hurt?' asked one.

'Me lying flat on the blanket should give you a clue,' groaned Gordon, who had recovered consciousness again.

'I meant how many. Anyone else?'

'If you could have a quick look at Elsie?' asked Ken. 'She went in after him.'

'No, I'm fine,' she said. 'I didn't get so much as a splinter.'

'Come over to the ambulance,' the medic insisted. 'Sometimes you don't notice a knock until afterwards. Best to be sure.'

'What was all that about 112 instead of 999?' Ken asked Martin as the medic looked into Elsie's eyes and asked her who the current prime minister was.

'Oh, if you can't get reception from your own provider,' said Martin, '112 will connect you to another one if there is a signal from it in the area. I think the location can also be traced, in case you are lost.'

'Good grief, I never knew that.'

'Will Gordon be OK?' Elsie asked anxiously a few minutes later when she was given the all clear.

The medic looked across at his colleague, who raised a thumb.

'He'll be fine. Is there someone to take you home? You really shouldn't drive.'

'I'll be doing that,' said Ken.

'Good. Now if you feel strange in any way. Sick, dizzy, anything, just see your GP or come to A&E.'

'I really am fine,' Elsie assured him as Gordon, now sporting a bandage round his head, was wheeled to the ambulance.

'See what a mess you've made of our shed?' he said to her as he was helped into the ambulance. 'They'll take it out of your wages you know.' Then, reaching out and taking her hand, 'Thanks Elsie. I'll never forget what you've done.'

'Come on,' said Ken, helping her to the car. 'Home, I think. You've just saved someone's life. But my God how nearly you lost your own.'

'I really feel one of you now,' she said happily.

'You were already one of us,' he said.

17

I often wondered why Ellen Willmott never married. I suppose in those days men were definitely in charge and she wouldn't have liked that. I wouldn't have minded though, and I'd have enjoyed looking after you.

Ellen Willmott was fascinated by all plants. She had been elected to the Royal Horticultural Society narcissus committee many years before and was deeply involved in the breeding of new strains of daffodil, but her magnum opus, *The Genus Rosa,* demonstrated her love for this particular plant perhaps more than any other. Her prize rose collection, together with an assortment of figs and grapes, grew in the secluded gardens of Wellmead, across the main Brentwood Road and a little to the south. The roses had been severely set back by one particular tenant a few years before and they were only now beginning to recover their former glory.

She stopped and smiled at the little patch of land by the lane leading from the main road. Jacob Maurer had taken it over to grow potatoes, the garden of South Lodge being taken up with other vegetables in addition to fruit bushes and flowers. She knew he needed to grow them to help to feed his large family and did not begrudge it to him – as long as he tended it in his own time of course. He walked over each morning and evening to earth them up, to deal with any weeds and if necessary to water them, and often wheeled a load back in his barrow assisted by one of his children.

It was well past six o'clock in the evening as she passed through the main gate of Warley Place and saw Jacob about to enter his cottage. He doffed his hat at her and she bade him good day, then stopped for a moment as Iris, his youngest daughter, toddled out to greet him. She watched as he bent to pick her up, smoothing her hair and giving her a kiss.

She walked on a few steps and saw another figure walking along the main road towards her gardener's cottage. It looked like young Maggie Saywood, the daughter of the couple who ran the bothy, and she turned again to see Jacob put Iris down and let the little girl go to meet the new arrival. A small parcel, gift-wrapped, changed hands and she heard the child cry out with excitement. Perhaps it was her birthday; Ellen Willmott had no idea, she didn't bother much with such things. She saw Jacob and Maggie smiling at each other.

But as she walked on she felt some irritation. Jacob had worked from six o'clock that morning, as usual, and now over twelve hours later he could still be cheerful. He had too many children for the accommodation he had been allocated and not enough money to feed or clothe them properly and yet they always appeared clean, neat and tidily dressed and never hungry.

She walked a little faster but felt an empty feeling inside. She had everything she could want; her music, with the very best musical instruments that money could buy; she had her printing press, her telescope, her camera, her books; a house that most people could never even dream of, and was visited by royalty. Jacob had none of these things, but still he was content. His wife had died, but he had two women looking after him, his cousin and a local girl whose friendship was, in her opinion, perhaps lacking in propriety. She would have to have a word with him about that.

She certainly did not want a man in her life, not one that would need looking after and would undoubtedly do his best to interfere with her work. And as for children, it was too late for that, but anyway they too would have just got in the way. No, she was better off as she was. There was a time when she had wondered about a relationship but no one suitable was available. Later on she had wondered about the doctor but, good a companion as he was, she knew that would almost certainly change if they became a couple. He was no different from any man and would treat her possessions as if they were his own and start giving her advice, or even telling her what to do. At least she could vote now, on account of her property. A lot of women couldn't though. It was true that they probably wouldn't really understand what they were voting for, but then neither would most men.

Her knees were beginning to ache as she reached the top of the sloping carriage drive and she was relieved, but at the same time irritated at being so, on reaching the turning circle and level ground. The house came into view; its columned entrance porch, with no fewer than three windows on either side, seven above that and a further three on the third floor, was certainly impressive. A house like that, surrounded by gardens such as these, no wonder people came to visit from far and wide – influential people, too.

She walked round the back and let herself in through the conservatory, as was her custom. Glancing briefly at the mahonia growing against the north wall, she went on into the music room intending to play one of her Amati violins to soothe her troubled mind. Getting as far as picking one up, she was unable to raise the enthusiasm to do more than draw the bow once across the strings before setting it down. Contenting herself for a while with admiring the many instruments of great worth surrounding her, she suddenly went quickly on into the staircase corridor, her footsteps echoing in the otherwise empty building. Should she immerse herself in her darkroom for an hour or so? Should she sit and read in her library? Needlework? What was the matter? Why couldn't she make up her mind? Why did nothing interest her this day?

She turned on her heel and strode out the way she had come and then to her walled garden, where she sat on a bench in the fading light to be with her plants.

Her irritable mood gradually softened, but still the thought kept coming back to her. Jacob Maurer: why was he always so bloody happy?

18

I had never thought about how people would react to any success I might have. Since I'd never had any, I'd never had the chance to find out. I was really shocked at what happened when my picture appeared in the paper. I was convinced it would be best for all of us if we called it a day.

Elsie stood there, dumbfounded.

'You're not going back, and that's final,' her father stormed, throwing the newspaper down.

Elsie picked it up. There, on the front page, was a picture of her being pulled out of the wreckage of the hut, face dirty, eyes wide. Underneath was the picture of the hut taken, as the caption said, seconds later. It had been flattened completely.

'HEROINE', was the headline. Then, underneath the pictures, 'Heroine Elsie Clark rescues trapped volunteer at Warley Place.'

She read a few lines before putting it down.

'You know how papers exaggerate things.'

'Them pictures, they don't lie,' said her father. 'You ain't going back, that's an end to it.'

'Mum?' pleaded Elsie to her mother.

'Well your father's right, it does look rather dangerous,' her mother agreed.

'When you read about someone getting knocked down on the road you don't stop going out, do you?'

'That's different,' said her father.

'I'm twenty years old,' said Elsie. 'I can do what I want.'

'Not when you're living in my house.'

'Then I'll stop living in your house.'

'What, and go and live with your fancy man?' said her father. 'The one that lets you get into danger like that? Why didn't he go in, that's what I'd like to know? Don't know why you want to mix with them high-falutin' do-gooders anyway.'

'They couldn't get in because the opening was too small for any of them,' she cried, tears now starting to form. 'Ken told me to stay out and wait for the firemen. And they aren't 'high-falutin' do-gooders' as you put it. They are ordinary decent people and I like them.'

'But he didn't stop you, did he!'

'I was too quick for him. If he'd tried he could have brought the lot down.'

'Oh yes?'

There was a knock at the door and her mother hurried out.

'It's Jamie,' she called. 'Come on in Jamie.'

Elsie swore under her breath as he walked in. Devious-looking eyes, hair hanging down over his forehead, white unhealthy pallor, she couldn't believe that she ever went out with him.

'Long time no see,' whined Jamie.

'Yes.'

'Sit down Jamie, I'll get some tea brewing.'

Elsie's mother disappeared into the kitchen.

With her father sitting in the only single chair Elsie had little option but to sit on the sofa, quickly joined by Jamie. His BO hadn't improved, she noticed. Only then did her father get up.

'I'm off out,' he muttered, getting his jacket from the banister on the way out. 'Nothing but trouble since you got involved in that lot,' he called from the front door.

'See you're in the paper then Else.'

She hated being called Else, especially by Jamie.

'Yes.'

'Quite the hero then?'

'Heroine. Not really. The papers always make it seem more than it is.'

'I suppose so. Fancy coming out tonight then? Pictures p'raps?'

'Jamie, I've got a boyfriend.'

'Yeah, seen his car. Don't mean you can't see yer old mates though, eh?'

'Jamie, the last time we saw each other all you wanted to do was to feel my tits as I recall.'

'Well, so what? Don't expect I was the first.'

'You weren't the first to try it.'

'Oh, the first to succeed then? Not much meat under them though, is there?'

140

He lifted his head and tried to peer down the front of her top, foiled by the high neck of her blouse.

'Jamie, I've just had a row with my mother and father. I don't want one with you as well. Thanks for coming, but it's time to go. I've got work soon anyway.'

'Still doing the old cleaning then?'

'Yes, and what's wrong with that?'

'Nothing, just asking. Sorry, didn't mean to upset you.'

He slid one arm round her waist and pulled her to him. He put the other hand on her stomach. She felt it slip under her blouse and start sliding upwards, while his face turned towards her, wet mouth open. Perhaps this was it. This was her world, the one she was born to inhabit?

'No it bloody well isn't!' she cried, pushing him away and getting to her feet.

'What yer bleedin' talking about?' he said, puzzled and annoyed.

She stared at him until, glaring back, he rose to his feet and made for the door.

'Dunno what you're on about. You're getting too big for yer boots, you are,' he said vehemently. 'You need to remember where yer roots are; where you belong.'

She shut the front door behind him and nearly knocked the tray from her mother's hands as, crying tears of anger and frustration, she dashed upstairs to her room.

As she lay on her bed her sobbing gradually subsided. Was he right? Were they all right? Was she really getting too high and mighty? She only knew a world of boozing, watching the soaps, letting the boyfriend have a grope on the sofa and, from what her friends told her, a lot more in the bedroom when the parents were out. God she was a fool to think things could ever be any different.

There was a tap on the door.

'Elsie dear?'

Elsie sat up and wiped her eyes.

'Yes mum. Come in.'

'Oh dear, what have we come to, quarrelling like this. We only want the best for you.'

'You do mum. Not sure about dad.'

'Him too. He's not very good at showing it though. He doesn't understand what you are getting into. It frightens him. He's seen what happens to people when they try to move out of their class.'

'Who does he know that's done that?'

'Well, on the tele, I mean.'

'And you? What do you really think?'

'I'm worried for you too.'

'There's only one person who can stop me spending the rest of my life with Ken,' said Elsie firmly. 'And that's Ken.'

'Ken is a good man,' said her mother. 'A very good man. He won't want to hurt you so he'll stay with you for that reason alone, if for no other. It will be up to you to do what is best for both of you.'

Elsie felt a sinking feeling in her stomach.

'Are you sure that's where you belong Elsie? In Ken's world? Do you think you'll ever fit in there?'

'Mum, Ken's family had little more than we have when they started. They have working class roots, they aren't upper class toffs.'

'But they've moved on. What do his parents think? You've met them, do they really accept you?'

Elsie didn't reply. She didn't know what to think any more.

'I've got to go to work now,' she said. 'We'll talk some more when I get back.'

'Please don't cry,' said her mother.

Elsie got changed quickly. She didn't like the evening shift. Mornings were OK, but she was tired in the evening. Still, it was a job. Some of them did a full day job and cleaned in the evening as well.

A car pulled up alongside as she started walking. For a moment she thought it was Ken, but Jamie had borrowed his brother's car.

'Lift Elsie?'

'Thanks, but I like a walk.'

He didn't say anything, just started to wind the window up.

'Jamie,' she said before it shut. 'I'm sorry about earlier. I'd just had a row with my parents. It wasn't your fault.'

'No problem,' he said casually, but she could see he was pleased.

Oh God, she thought. He'll probably take that apology for an invitation to come back and have another grope so he can go and boast to his mates.

She managed to put the row behind her as she walked to the office. Several people did a second take as she walked past, no doubt wondering where they had seen her before. God it must be awful being a celebrity, she thought, with people staring at you all the time. Or perhaps they like it?

The security man let her in.

'Great thing you did there,' he said. 'You must be proud. Don't think I could have done it.'

'I think you would,' said Elsie. 'You don't get time to think about it. But yes, you would have done.'

He looked pleased.

She went to the cupboard to collect her cleaning things.

'Oh, we are honoured,' said Kelly, doing a curtsey. 'A heroine in our midst.'

'Knock it off Kelly, I've had a rotten day so far.'

'Tell us about it at tea Elsie?'

'There's not much to tell, Pam. You know newspapers.'

Ruby and Mary didn't say anything.

It was good, getting stuck into cleaning. You could forget your problems. Nothing to worry about. Move the mouse pad, move the diary (that should have been put away), squirt the polish, quick rub; next desk. Her problems were soon a thing of the past. Yes, this was where she belonged. Wasn't it?

'Elsie!'

The call came from the stairwell.'

'Right Pam, coming!'

She walked down to where Pam had made the tea.

'Right,' said Pam when they were sitting down, steaming cups in front of them. 'Tell us all about it?'

'There's nothing to tell,' said Elsie. 'You know the way papers exaggerate things. Gordon was out cold in the shed, I helped – '

'No, not that you idiot,' said Ruby. 'We can read, can't we?'

'No Ruby,' Pam broke in nervously, 'That is what – '

'Ken,' said Ruby. 'Has he got you in bed yet? What's he like, any good?'

'Hey, he doesn't get you to dress up, does he?' said Kelly. 'A nurse. I bet it's a nurse. Or a cleaning lady? Does he like you tickling him with your duster?'

'No,' protested Elsie.

'Oh, he doesn't get you to dress up? Oh well, never mind, as long as he does it.'

'How big is his – '

'No!' broke in Pam.

' – house,' continued Ruby, grinning. 'I mean, is he rich?'

'What will you do when the baby comes?' asked Kelly.

Elsie burst into tears.

There was silence for a moment.

'My God, she *is* pregnant,' said Kelly.

'I'm not, I'm not,' sobbed Elsie. 'It's been a bloody awful day and I could do without this.'

Pam put her arm round Elsie's shoulders.

'Don't cry pet, they don't mean any harm.'

'That's right,' said Mary. 'Don't mind us. It's just our bloody silly way of coping with life.'

'It's not you, you've been good mates. If only that man hadn't taken the photographs.'

'I bet he got a good price for them, too,' said Kelly. 'You do the dangerous bit and get sod all, he takes some snaps and makes a mint.'

'My mum and dad have told me not to go any more.'

'Don't take any notice of them,' said Pam. 'We've never seen you happier than when you met Ken.'

'And they want me to give Ken up. They might be right.'

'No,' said Ruby. 'Bollocks to them. Tell them from me.'

'My dad thinks I'm getting ideas above my station,' Elsie said.

'Someone might end up getting hurt,' said Mary philosophically. 'But it will be fun while it lasts.'

Somehow her friends' support had the opposite effect and by the time she was walking back home she knew what she had to do. Not because of the accident, not exactly. She belonged with those she knew. Her mum and dad knew it, her friends knew it, Ken's mother knew it and his father probably did but was trying not to show it. Nothing but hurt could come of it all. She didn't mind getting hurt herself. Well, perhaps she did, actually. But

144

even more the hurt it could bring to her parents, and most of all to Ken. Her eyes filled with tears. It had to end. She had to finish it.

When she got home she picked up the phone.

'Ken,' she said. 'There's something I need to say to you. Not over the phone. Can we meet somewhere?'

19

I wonder how many of Ellen Willmott's gardeners went off to the war and how many of them came back. It must have been awful for them and so good, if they did make it home, to return to the peace of the garden.

Jacob was locking the big wooden door to the filmy fern cave when he heard his name being called.

'Papa! Papa!'

It was John, his son, the oldest one there while Max was away in Switzerland. They were not allowed in the garden unless they were working under his supervision so he quickly scrambled along the side of the pond to access the path to the bridge. He relaxed a little when he saw Alfie break from his work and go up to the boy. Alfie saw Jacob approaching and pointed to him.

'Papa, that man is here again and he is waiting for you.'

'What man?' asked a puzzled Jacob.

'That man who was here before. The one that was a soldier.'

'Felix Martinsyde?'

'Yes, that was his name.'

'I wasn't expecting him. Were you?' he asked Alfie, who shook his head.

'Very well John, you run along and tell him we'll be along directly,' Jacob said to his son. 'You may as well come too Alfie,' he added. 'It may be you he has come to see and the end of the day is near.'

They walked back across the bridge and down the path to the drive, both deep in thought oblivious to the rhododendrons in all their beauty and the mallards on the pond as they made their way to Jacob's cottage. Felix Martinsyde was waiting outside.

'Hello again Mr Martinsyde,' greeted Jacob, stretching out his hand.

'Hello Mr Maurer, thank-you for seeing me. Hello again Alfie.'

'Good to see you sir.'

'Felix,' Martinsyde said with a grimace.

'Sorry sir, don't seem right somehow.'

146

Jacob smiled as he led them through the gate to his back garden.

'It's a bit crowded in there,' he explained.

'This is fine,' said his guest.

'Did you come for a look round the gardens?' asked Jacob. 'Or to see Miss Willmott?'

'No, lovely though the first would be and honoured though I would be to do the second, it's you I came to see.'

Jacob and Alfie waited in silence while, brow furrowed, Martinsyde collected himself.

'When I left the army,' he said eventually, 'things were rather difficult.'

'So I 'eard,' said Alfie. 'Bloody disgrace it was too.'

Jacob laid a hand on Alfie's arm to silence him.

'Alfie used to talk so fondly of his life in these gardens and of his plants – he saw them as his, even if they belonged to Miss Willmott.'

'Yes,' said Jacob, 'we all think of the plants as ours.'

'You know I was court-martialled after the war?'

'Alfie did mention it,' said Jacob.

'I still don't understand sir,' said Alfie, unable to keep quiet. 'You saved all our lives. Those Hun machine guns would have mowed us all down. Walking up to them like that, no gun in your hand, you wasn't to know that Hun officer would have taken any notice.'

'I simply assumed that the Germans were basically the same as us, Alfie. In fact I was sure they were and that their officer would also be aware of the approaching end to the conflict. He wouldn't have wanted the killing to continue any more than I did. There was very little risk. In fact since I would have been killed anyway there was no additional risk at all.'

'Well it was still a very brave thing to do sir and it saved all our lives. It was a stupid order in the first place.'

'That's as may be Alfie, but we have to do what we are told to do in war, like it or not. If you don't you have to take the consequences, as I had to. Anyway, as I was saying, everywhere I went for employment they wanted to see my service record.'

'And there was the court martial?' said Jacob.

'There was the court martial. I couldn't get a job. I had a little capital, not much and I was eating into it to live, but enough to start a small business. I wanted the peace and contentment of which Alfie spoke so often so I decided to start a plant nursery.'

'That's a bit different from gardening,' said Jacob.

'Yes, but it involved plants and that was enough for me at the time.'

'How did you get the plants?' asked Jacob, with an awful feeling that he already knew the answer.

'A lot of them came from one of Alfie's wartime friends who had proved extremely good at scrounging anything we wanted,' said Martinsyde. 'A chap called Wally Barnes.'

Jacob looked at Alfie, who was sitting there with his mouth open and eyes wide.

'I really didn't know where he was getting them from then,' continued Martinsyde. 'First it was snowdrops, daffodils, crocuses, that sort of thing. The plants themselves in the spring, bulbs at other times. Then some other plants that he didn't know the names of. That's when I began to suspect, so I made a few enquiries and paid you a visit.'

'So that's why you came?'

'Yes, and it confirmed what I thought. He was getting them from here. He said he could get some really special plants and he would have their names. I was going to tell him our deal was at an end but I don't think he would have been that easy to put off. Anyway, he never turned up with the plants and I haven't seen him since. What I don't know is whether he will turn up again.'

'I don't think you will have any trouble on that score sir,' said Alfie. 'I crossed swords with him and he won't be back.'

'Well that's a relief,' said the officer. 'How did you – no, perhaps I don't want to know.'

'Well you can carry on your business in peace now,' said Jacob.

'Not exactly. Barnes had told his wife about me, told her I was part of his thievery and when he didn't come home she told the police. They are making enquiries at the moment and once they speak to Miss Willmott I expect they'll do me for it.'

'And that will be the end of your dream?' said Jacob.

'That will be the end of my dream.'

'Wait a minute,' said Alfie. 'That's not fair.'

'Fair or not, no one is above the law.'

'But if no one wants to prosecute you surely they will drop it?'

'Alfie, if Ellen Willmott finds out people have been stealing her plants she will want to prosecute,' said Jacob.

'Well, I just wanted to apologise for being so stupid as to get involved in this,' said Martinsyde. 'Now I will be on my way.'

'No, wait,' protested Alfie. 'I wouldn't be here if it wasn't for you. I'll say I done it.'

'I bought and sold stolen goods, it's as simple as that.'

'I don't think it is that simple,' said Jacob, 'but I don't see how we can help, Alfie. Miss Willmott isn't going to let it go.'

'If you tell her that Mr Martinsyde just found out what Barnes was doing and that he tried to put a stop to it, she won't want to take it any further. Not if it means a British officer is involved,' Alfie pleaded to Jacob.

'She'll want someone to blame.'

'Then blame me. Say I was involved but stopped Barnes when he went for her really good stuff. She can sack me, honour satisfied and the Lieutenant can carry on with his business. I can soon find another job.'

'No,' said Martinsyde. 'How do you think I would feel if someone else took the blame for my stupidity?'

'May I suggest that we speak to Miss Willmott about this?' suggested Jacob. 'After all, she is going to hear about it sooner or later and best coming from you I would think. It will be her decision in the end.'

'You are right Jacob,' said Martinsyde.

'John,' called Jacob to his son. 'Run up and tell Robinson that we would like to speak to Miss Willmott about a matter of some importance, will you? We will follow directly.'

As John sped up the hill they slowly got to their feet to follow him. They made their way up the drive, Alfie staring gloomily at the ground, the lieutenant biting his lip and Jacob with his brow furrowed in thought.

'She will see you in the conservatory,' said Robinson, meeting them as they reached the turning circle at the front of the big house.

Ellen Willmott was watering her mahonia when they got to the door. She glanced at them and finished what she was doing before addressing them.

'Well what is it that is so important that you have to disturb me at this hour and who are you sir?'

'This is Mr Martinsyde ma'am,' broke in Alfie while Jacob looked at him aghast. 'He's a very brave man who saved me and my mates' lives in the war. Deserves a bloody medal – beg your pardon – but got nothing. We was – '

'Thank-you Alfie,' said Miss Willmott. 'I don't think we need detain you any further.'

'But – '

'Off you go Alfie,' said Jacob. 'I think Miss Willmott has got the message.'

'Come in then,' she said, waving to chairs by a little table on which a jug of orange juice stood with some glasses. Would you like a drink, either of you?'

They both thanked her and Robinson poured them a glass each before leaving the room.

'Well, now we can have a more conventional introduction,' she said.

'I really must apologise for interrupting your work,' said Felix Martinsyde. 'I was a Lieutenant at the end of the war and Alfie was under my command. An excellent soldier he was too, saving my life on one occasion.'

'And what is this about you saving theirs?'

'Just one of those things that happens in war,' he answered.

'No Miss Willmott,' said Jacob. 'It was not one of those things. Alfie told me all about it.'

He recounted what had happened when the platoon was asked to carry out the suicidal charge and the resulting court martial.

'Is all this true?' she asked Martinsyde when Jacob had finished.

He nodded.

'But many people did many brave things,' he said. 'I saw some of those young pilots flying over enemy territory day after day knowing that they may soon be falling in flames while we were safe on the ground.'

'Hardly safe, I would have thought,' she said dryly.

She was quiet for a moment, deep in thought. Jacob knew quite well that she was thinking of just such an airman.

'Very well,' she said eventually. 'We have established your credentials. What brings you here?'

'I have done a stupid thing,' he said. 'Unable to gain employment after the war I decided to start a plant nursery.'

'An excellent choice.'

'I thought so. But I made a grave error of judgement. I employed one of my ex-soldiers to obtain plants for me to sell. He was stealing them.'

'Not Alfie!' she said.

'No, not Alfie. He would never have done such a thing. It was a man called Barnes. I understand from Jacob here that you caught him on one occasion and gave him the fright of his life.'

'Ah yes, I remember.'

'I should have known that he could have been stealing them from here, but I was having difficulty getting the business going and simply didn't ask the right questions or make the necessary enquiries. So, although I cannot be certain, it seems that I may have inadvertently been selling your bulbs.'

'Did you know this, Jacob?'

'No. He apparently only took bulbs from the daffodil bank and such places where they would not be missed. None of your hybrids were disturbed.'

'So where is the wretched man now?'

'We don't know,' said Felix.

'There is more,' continued Jacob. 'Just a few days ago Barnes threatened Alfie that he would get his own back and do grave harm to you if he didn't help him get some more expensive plants. He had a rather large knife with which he would carry out this threat. So one night Alfie showed him where the plants were.'

She was quiet for a minute; going over his previous short conversation with her, Jacob surmised. It was as well he had told her then what he knew.

'Barnes said if he told anyone then he would kill you or me instead.'

'So what happened? How many plants did they take? I have not noticed any missing.'

'I disturbed them and Barnes was going to carry out his threat. Alfie stopped him.'

'Stopped him? How?'

'I think it would be better if you did not know any more ma'am, other than that Alfie had both our interests at heart, however misguided he may have been in his actions. Before that day he had no part in the misappropriation of any of the items Mr Martinsyde has mentioned.'

'So where is Barnes now?'

'Neither of us knows,' said Jacob. Felix nodded in agreement. 'I think Alfie may know more but I would prefer not to know,' he continued. 'But I believe him when he said he will not bother any of us again.'

'Well, what a situation,' she said.

'The police are involved,' said Felix, explaining about the note Barnes had left his wife.

'Oh dear.'

She lapsed into thought.

'Right,' she said eventually. 'There has been enough suffering in that awful war and you have been treated abominably. You have been naive and Alfie has been misguided in my opinion. I will simply tell the police that none of my plants are missing and that although he may have wanted to steal them he was prevented by my vigilance. He was obviously too ashamed at having a woman thwart him that he invented a cock and bull story to save his pride.'

'They may be able to trace some of the plants back to you, Miss Willmott,' warned Felix.

'I don't see how, but if they do then we'll just say I sold some to you. Can you give Robinson a list of some sort so that he can make out some bills of sale Jacob?'

Jacob nodded.

'And you can get on with your business, Mr Martinsyde.'

'I really don't know how to thank you, Miss Willmott.'

She thought for a moment.

'Well there is one thing you can do.'

'Anything.'

'You can sell my plants and seeds for me. I will let you have them at a reasonable price. You can pay me when you have sold them, so you'll not have to lay out a large amount.'

'You are too kind.'

'Jacob can sort the plants out. Have you any botanical experience?'

'Only what I've gleaned over the past year. There is such a lot to learn.'

'In that case Alfie can help you. Jacob will sort out the details. If you do well then I would not stand in the way of Alfie joining you, I am sure he is more than capable.'

'I am very much obliged.'

She nodded and turned away.

Felix Martinsyde looked at Jacob who inclined his head towards the door and they quietly rose and left while Ellen Willmott carried on tending to her plants.

'That's not the Ellen Willmott that I have heard about,' he said once they were well out of earshot.

'She knew a young airman once,' said Jacob. 'She feels she let him down. Perhaps she is trying to make up for that; perhaps not. You can never quite read what is in her mind.'

20

I was so glad when you refused to take any notice and insisted on carrying on seeing me! And didn't you do it in style? I really thought it was over, you and me. Life suddenly seemed empty. It was like waking from a lovely dream, or coming home from a holiday. But I should have known. But asking me to marry you, I could hardly believe it. Then to cap it all, there was the walnut tree.

Ken drove up to Elsie's house not really knowing what to do. He tried to understand what she was going through, being unable to make her mind up about their relationship. Perhaps she was flattered but wanted to stick to what she knew. If that was the case, was he being fair to her? Should he simply accept what she said and move on? But surely he couldn't have been that wrong in believing that she thought just as much of him as he did of her?

It had been awful, that scene. Not wanting to accept what she said, but not wanting to hurt her either. She'd made him take her boots back, her rucksack, the gloves – everything he had bought her. It would have been too painful to keep them, she'd said. She'd cried all right, but been insistent that it was for the best.

The next few days had been grim. He'd been honest with his parents, told them what had happened. His mother had looked relieved and his father said he'd support him whatever Ken decided, but he was sorry it had come to that. He'd had some doubts about it though, he'd added.

He got out of the car, opened the boot and got out his rucksack. It had a little folding seat attached to it, useful for tea breaks at Warley when there were not enough logs to sit on. Several of the volunteers had them.

Carrying it in one hand, he went to the door and knocked. Elsie's mother answered it, looking a little frightened and a little relieved.

'Could I have a quick word with Elsie,' he asked. 'I'm not here to make a scene.'

Elsie's father appeared from the lounge.

'She don't want to see you,' he said.

Ken ignored him and spoke again to Mrs Clark.

'Please? At least ask her.'

'It's all right, I'm coming,' came Elsie's voice and a white faced figure came slowly down the stairs.

'I'm sorry Ken, I meant it.'

'I know you did. But I thought I'd just let you know that I'll be sitting here outside until you change your mind. I have some refreshments, but I might need to use the toilet in a couple of hours, if that's all right.'

He promptly unfolded the seat,sat down, pulled a thermos flask out and started to pour himself a drink.

'Clear off,' said Mr Clark.

'Can't do that I'm afraid.'

'D'you want me to make you?'

'Please don't try it.'

He looked at the three of them; the father, trying to pluck up the courage to get rid of him; the mother frightened and not knowing what to do – and Elsie. Elsie, tears coming now, but Elsie laughing.

'Get up Ken,' she said. 'Please. I'm not bending down there!'

He got to his feet and she threw herself at him, grabbing him so tightly he gasped for breath.

'I'm not going to be able to get rid of you, am I?'

'No, afraid not. Whatever problems we face, we'll get over them. Together. Come on Elsie, it's Monday. Time for work.'

'My things?' said Elsie.

'Are in the car,' said Ken. 'Together with sandwiches and drink.'

Elsie didn't say anything for a second, then turned and ran upstairs to change into her jeans.

'Everything is going to be fine,' Ken assured her parents as they stood there open-mouthed.

'Slow down!' called Ken as two minutes later Elsie reappeared and started to run down the stairs with her notebook.

'Would you really have just sat there?' she asked as they drove off.

'I didn't actually plan it,' said Ken. 'I didn't have a clue what I was going to do. All I knew is that I wasn't going to leave without you, so I guess the answer is yes, I would have done.'

155

He was silent as he negotiated a roundabout, then 'I want to marry you, Elsie Clark. I want to marry you as soon as we can arrange it. Say you will?'

She sat there for a moment, her mouth open, stunned.

'Please?' he said.

'Ken, are you sure?'

'Of course I'm sure.'

'I think we should wait until you really are sure.'

'I'm really sure that I'm really sure,' he said.

'I don't know what to say,' she said. 'Yes sounds so inadequate, but yes, of course, it's more than I could have ever dreamed of.'

'Believe me, marrying you would make me every bit as happy,' he said. 'But you'll have to promise that you won't go crawling into any wrecked huts, playing with chainsaws or doing anything the remotest bit dangerous,' he said to her.

'I can't believe it,' she said. 'I just can't believe it. A few weeks ago we'd never even met, now you've asked me to marry you. Are you sure you wouldn't prefer me to just move in with you? It's what lots of people are doing, just to be certain they are right for each other.'

'No, I'm a bit old-fashioned I suppose. Anyway, I already am certain.'

'I'm so happy,' she said as he slowed the car and turned to pass through the already open gate.

She was still smiling as they came to a halt in the car park.

'Blimey, you're both looking pleased with yourselves,' said Ben. 'We'll soon put a stop to that!'

Elsie looked at Ken.

'We're going to get married,' he said.

'What? Crikey, that's a first, two volunteers getting married. That's brilliant. Hey, you're not going to stop coming then, are you?'

'What's this?' asked Daphne, turning her head. 'Did I hear correctly?'

'You did,' confirmed Elsie.

'Oh I'm so glad. Shame we're not registered for weddings here!'

Suddenly they were surrounded by volunteers showering them with congratulations.

'Right,' said Ben eventually. 'A special occasion like this demands a special job.'

'Good grief!' groaned Ken. 'More logs to move?'

'No, something else. The walnut tree.'

'You want us to move the walnut tree?'

'No, you silly bugger. You know the concrete is breaking up at the top? Well it needs to be chipped away back to the firm stuff, then made good. You and Elsie can have a go at that if you like. You can do the heavy work, she can keep an eye on you!'

'Great,' said Elsie. 'That sounds fascinating.'

'Oh no!' laughed Ken. 'I was just going to go to the store to get the tools and a wheelbarrow! And there isn't one!'

'Have you looked?'

'Good God!' exclaimed Ken. There, under the now much smaller tree, stood a brand new shed.

'We don't hang about here you know,' said Ben grinning.

'The chap that took the photos got the Gazette to make a nice donation for a new one,' explained Daphne, 'and a few of us came down during the week to put it up.'

'I'll be there in a minute,' said Ben as Ken loaded the wheelbarrow with tools, threw the rucksacks on top, and he and Elsie started up the carriage drive to the walnut tree.

'Sure you wouldn't like to do some pointing with me on the terrace wall Elsie?' asked Carla as she joined them in the walk up the drive. 'No, stupid question,' she continued as she looked at the two of them. 'Well let me know when you're starting to re-concrete it, I'd like to see it being done.'

'Sure Carla,' said Ken. 'Probably about tea-break time, I wouldn't have thought there was a lot to be taken off.'

They broke off before they got to the start of the ha-ha wall and made their way across the meadow to the tree. Not only was it held up by the concrete put in during Ellen Willmott's time, the branches were also braced by a system of ties. The Essex Wildlife Trust wasn't going to let this particular tree go without doing everything they could to stop it falling down.

As they got closer to the tree Ken glanced at Elsie and put the barrow down.

'Are you all right?' he asked. 'You've gone very quiet.'

Elsie shivered a little and pulled her anorak tighter.

'I'm OK. It just feels strange, that's all. I don't know why.'

'If you'd rather – '

'No,' she broke in. 'I want to.'

They walked on and put the wheelbarrow down close to the tree underneath its spreading branches.

'Good grief,' commented Ken 'Look at that. Ben has been busy. He thinks of everything.'

The top of the concrete was about two metres from the ground and Ben had already prepared a platform out of wooden supports and scaffolding planks to enable them to reach it.

'Right,' said Ken rummaging about in the wheelbarrow. 'What have we got? Hard hat for a start.'

He passed a hat of the sort used in building sites to Elsie, who expertly twisted her long black hair and enclosed it inside the hat as she put it on.

'Goggles and gloves. That should do it.'

He put his own protective gear on too and pulled out a hammer, then helped Elsie up onto the planks.

The concrete was in even worse state than they had envisaged and when the bucket was full of rubble Ken got down to empty it into the barrow.

'There's a bigger bit here,' she called down to him. 'I'll just push it down, you'd better stand back.'

There was silence for a moment.

'I think you'd better get up here Ken.'

He climbed back on to the platform and looked where her finger was pointing.

The skeletal remains of a hand, down past the wrist, were protruding from where the concrete had broken away.

'Strewth! You said you had a strange feeling about it and it seems you were right. But aren't women supposed to scream and faint when they find something like this?'

'If it was moving I probably would,' she said.

'We'll have to call the police; they'll know what to do. I'll get Ben and Frank, they can ring them. I wish I had my camera, though I suppose they'll photograph it themselves. Do you want to come or will you be all right?'

'I'll stay here,' she said. 'I suppose they'll want to get the rest of the concrete off?'

'Oh, I suppose so. Best leave it alone for now.'

As he turned to leave he saw Ben coming towards him, accompanied by Gordon.

'Hey, look what we've found,' he called. 'What are you doing here?' he added to the latter. 'You should be resting.'

'I couldn't stay home,' said Gordon. 'I've promised not to do anything strenuous so I thought I'd come and give you a hand.'

'We've already got one,' called Elsie from the platform.

'Yes, yes, I know, you've got two each, but – '

'No, we've got an extra one.'

'We've found a body,' explained Ken. 'Or the hand, anyway, sticking out of the concrete.'

'Oh yes, very good,' they both laughed.

'No, really, come and see.'

'Yes, sure you have,' said Ben. 'It's that girlfriend of his,' he went on to explain to Gordon. 'He hasn't been right since he met her.'

They reached the tree and climbed up to look.

'Blimey,' said Ben. 'You weren't joking, were you?'

'Hi Elsie,' said Gordon, who had thanked her endlessly when he came out of hospital. 'Crikey. Have you tried the kiss of life?'

'Don't think it works through the fingers,' said Elsie solemnly. 'Wait till we uncover his mouth.'

'Perhaps it was Ellen Willmott's way of cementing a relationship with one of her admirers,' suggested Gordon.

'If you've finished with the jokes could you go and fetch Frank?' Ben asked him. 'I'll ring the police. Good grief Elsie, we've had nothing but excitement since you came. It'll be too much for some of these old fellas.'

'Just a suggestion Ben,' said Gordon. 'If you do ring them, just say you've found a body. If they think it's been there for eighty years we'll be waiting all day for them.'

'I think I might just say we've found some human remains,' Ben said. 'That should do it.'

He thumbed his mobile and was soon talking to someone. Then, clicking his phone off, he clipped it back in his belt.

'Apparently this has to be treated as a crime scene,' he grinned. 'We have to move away and be careful not to contaminate any forensic evidence that may be here.'

Gordon got down from the platform.

'I don't think much of this tree's chances by the time the police have finished,' he said. 'Mind you, it's not doing too well anyway.' He looked at some fungus at the base and picked at the bark. 'Its bark is worse than its blight,' he muttered as he walked off to find Frank.

'I think I'll ring the Gazette too,' said Ben. 'You might as well be headline news again Elsie!'

'Don't you dare,' she said. 'We can say Ken found it.'

'What, and pervert the course of justice? My goodness, the boys in blue are here already.'

A flashing blue light was making its way up the drive and the car itself came into view as it crested the rise and reached the turning circle. It stopped and they saw Gordon and Frank walking up to it, then pointing their way. Two policemen emerged and came towards them, stopping at first and looking doubtfully at the wall of the ha-ha before clambering down. They made their way up the sloping side and hurried towards them.

'I'd say you two are the prime suspects,' said Ben. 'Don't worry, I'll come and visit you in jail.'

They waited as the party approached and waved the two young policemen to the platform.

'Up there lads,' said Ben.

They climbed up and looked at the hand.

'We thought from your message it was the remains of someone who died recently,' said one looking suspiciously at Ben.

'Oh, sorry, did I give you that impression?' he asked innocently.

The other officer grinned. 'Have you tried the kiss of – '

'We've already done that one,' broke in Gordon.

'Oh.'

'Do you want us to break the rest away?' suggested Frank.

'No, I think our people will do that.'

'Well I don't want you damaging the tree. It's valuable.'

'We'll be careful. Any idea how it might have happened?'

'Yes, I think so,' said Gordon. 'Ellen Willmott was a bit of a battleaxe but really liked this tree. We think it was about to fall down, so she got one of her gardeners to hold it up while she poured concrete round him.'

'Funny man, eh?'

'Well how would we know what happened?'

'OK, leave it with us. We might use some help from you, but under our supervision.' Then looking at Ken and Elsie, 'So you two found it?'

They nodded.

'Well could you stop for a while? Sergeant Adams will be here shortly and we'll need to take a statement.'

'Well we were planning to stay all morning anyway,' said Ken. 'We'll find another job to do, or maybe just have a stroll round and come back in, what, an hour?'

'That will be fine sir.'

'No point in starting another job,' said Ben. 'Why not have a look round and make a note of anything that needs doing?'

'Fancy having a look at the purple toothwort?' Ken asked.

'The what?'

'It's a parasite that grows off the roots of trees. Frank keeps telling me which ones, but I still forget.'

'Poplar, willow and alder,' said Ben. 'I think it might have all gone by now, but have a look anyway.'

They strolled off back down the drive and turned to climb the short slope up to the gorge, over the bridge, then took the short path towards the south hide. Ken pushed the bushes aside and held them back for Elsie as they searched the ground.

'No, it's gone,' said Ken. 'Shame, it looks so pretty. Still, we'll see it next year. I've got some photos at home, I'll show you them.'

He held her hand while they clambered down the slope and over the rocks to stand at the side of the south pond.

'To think Ellen Willmott almost certainly stood here once,' she said. 'Jacob Maurer too, I suppose.'

'Certainly they did, both of them.'

Elsie suddenly frowned.

'What is it?' Ken asked.

'That man, the one you said got sacked by your father. I'm sure I saw him just then, up near the bridge.'

Ken rolled his eyes.

'He just doesn't know when to stop. I'll speak to him.'

Elsie shuddered.

'No, please don't. I've got an awful feeling about it.'

'Well it's time we got back to the walnut tree anyway, and we have to go that way.'

He took her hand.

'Mrs Bradshaw; I can't wait to call you that.'

'Oh Ken, I'm so happy.'

They walked, arms round each other, along the short path and then let go to pass separately over the narrow bridge.

Ken heard hurried footsteps behind and turned just in time to see a hand with a rock in it coming down at his head, then a blinding pain and merciful oblivion.

21

But, my dearest Ken, with such a heavy heart I write this to say goodbye. A definite one this time. Your life was straightforward before you met me, but since then you've had nothing but problems, and now this. They say you might not recover. If you don't, then I won't recover either. Never. I'll miss you always. With love, Elsie.

How things have changed, Elsie thought. One day life is empty, the next full of happiness, full of promise. Life really is good.

She heard a thump from behind her, turned and screamed. That man, the one she saw from the lake, the one trying to blackmail the Bradshaws, was standing over the now still body. Blood was pouring from Ken's head and the brick was raised for another blow. In that second she saw her world falling apart, the end of all her dreams. But in that same second her instinct took over.

She curled her fingers into claws, screamed a scream not of fear but of rage, like a vixen defending her cubs, then launched herself at him. His eyes opened wide in surprise as she hit him. He staggered back and caught his feet on a rock. She kicked at his legs and the hard toe-caps of her boots contacted his shin. He cried out in pain and tried to draw his leg back, but prevented by the rock. Then, slowly, his arms wind-milling frantically trying to keep his balance, he toppled backwards into the gorge.

Else didn't wait to see what happened to him, she was down on her knees beside Ken. What she could see of his face past the blood was white and he didn't seem to be breathing. She filled her lungs with air and screamed for help. She was later told that they even heard it from the walnut tree.

She heard running feet and Donald appeared.

'He's killed him,' she sobbed. 'That man's killed my Ken.'

Donald pulled a handkerchief out, glancing down at the bottom of the gorge as he did so and seeing a body spread-eagled against a rock. From the angle of his head it was obvious his neck was broken.

He turned back to Ken and felt his skull through the blood to make sure it was not broken, then placed his handkerchief up against it.

'Press that against the wound,' he said. 'I'll call an ambulance.'

'What happened?' asked Donald, dialling 112. 'No, wait a second.'

He gave the emergency operator the details and explained that the police were already on the site.

'I was crossing the bridge,' she said, 'and that man came up behind us and hit Ken. I ran at him and kicked him to stop him hitting him again and he fell into the gorge.'

Peter came running up, closely followed by Robin, took one look at Ken and bent closely over his face, then put his fingers on Ken's neck.

'Peter's done a first aid course,' explained Donald. 'He'll sort Ken out until the ambulance gets here.'

'He's breathing, just,' Peter said, 'and he's got a pulse but it's rather weak. Can you go down and tell the ambulance men to bring a stretcher when they come, Donald?'

As he folded a handkerchief and pressed it against the wound he glanced down into the gorge.

'Who the hell's that?'

'He's the one that hit Ken,' said Donald. 'Elsie stopped him hitting him a second time and he fell down there.'

'Well he won't be attacking anyone else from the look of it,' Peter commented. 'But I'd better go down and have a look. Press on this, Robin, but not too hard in case his skull is fractured.'

Walking along to the shallower end of the gorge, he made his way back to the body. Bending over it he put his fingers to the neck and, looking up, shook his head before leaving the body and making his way back to the bridge.

Elsie had the feeling that she should be shocked that she had killed someone, but just felt numb. He had tried to kill Ken and had deserved whatever he had got. Even so, she had to push the panic down as it threatened to overwhelm her.

'Is he all right?' asked one of the policemen from the walnut tree, bent double and gasping after his climb up the steps from the drive.

'Not sure,' said Peter. 'He's alive, but goodness knows what's going on inside his head. If he's bleeding in there he needs to be in hospital right now.'

'I'll get the air ambulance,' said the policemen, then hearing the siren. 'No, they're here now. Jesus Christ, what's that?'

He had noticed the body in the gorge.

'It's the person who did this to Ken,' said Donald. 'Elsie here stopped him hitting him a second time. If he had done, Ken would have been dead for sure.'

'Is it always like this when you are around,' said the policeman. 'First a body in the tree, now one in the gorge. Hey, don't I know you?'

'Her picture was in the local paper,' explained Donald. 'She crawled into a hut and rescued – '

'Oh yes, I remember.'

Donald turned and ran down the steps to meet the ambulance while the policeman scrambled down into the gorge to check the body.

The enormity of what she had done suddenly struck Elsie. She had killed someone. It had been to save Ken getting battered again, to be sure, but nevertheless she had killed someone. What would they do to her? If Ken didn't recover then she didn't care, but if he did and she was in prison, she couldn't stand it. She started to shake.

'It's OK Elsie,' Peter said looking up at her. 'I think he'll be all right.'

The policeman climbed out of the gorge and spoke to Elsie.

'You'll need to make a statement,' he said. 'I know you've told me already, but he's dead so we have to be very clear exactly what happened.'

'Not now,' said Peter. 'You can see she's in shock.'

The policeman spoke into his radio, asking for SOCO to attend.

'Socko?' asked Elsie. 'Who's Socko?'

'It stands for Scene of Crime Officer,' explained the policeman. 'He needs to attend when a crime has been committed.'

'But I had to get him off Ken,' cried Elsie, aghast. 'I didn't do anything wrong.'

'Not you,' smiled the policeman. 'Him.'

He pointed to the body in the gorge.

'I'm sorry, it's all too much for me,' she gulped as Peter put his arm round her.

Donald appeared, followed by the ambulance men, with Frank and Ben behind them.

One of the paramedics bent over Ken while the other went down to check on the body.

'We need to get this one to hospital now,' he called to his colleague after examining Ken's head. 'He's still unconscious and we don't know what's happening in there. Pass me the collar.'

After fitting the collar and lifting him onto the stretcher, they started down the narrow steep path to the drive where the ambulance was waiting.

'About that statement,' said the policeman.

'I think she needs to be checked out first,' said Peter. 'They can do that in the ambulance, then you can take her statement at the hospital.'

'I'll come with you,' said Donald, pulling her back and letting the rest of the party go on ahead. 'What exactly happened?'

Elsie told him, choking back the tears.

'Right, that's almost what I saw. Except that although you ran at him, you didn't actually touch him. And I didn't see you kick him.'

'But I – '

'No, I think you are getting confused. You went to help Ken and that man lost his balance and fell down there. It was his own fault. You had nothing to do with it. If you say you pushed him or kicked him, goodness knows what will happen. You saved Ken's life, but a clever lawyer will present it differently and it won't help either you or Ken.'

'I understand,' she said. 'He will be all right, won't he?'

'I'm sure he will.'

They caught up with the group again and Elsie climbed up into the ambulance after Ken's stretcher, her boots making a clatter on the metal steps. Donald looked at her feet.

'I tell you what,' he suggested. 'If I can have Ken's car keys I'll get your rucksack and his, put them in my car and you can change into something more comfortable at the hospital. Also I can drive you back afterwards; Ken is certain to be kept in.'

'No, that's all right,' she said.

'Yes,' said Donald firmly.

Too confused to argue, Elsie put her hand in Ken's pocket and retrieved the car keys, passing them to Donald.

'See you there then.'

'Step on it Fred,' said the paramedic, opening one of Ken's eyelids and shining a torch into the eye.

The siren started up and the ambulance lurched slowly down the drive, then sped up as it turned into the main road.

'Please be all right Ken,' said Elsie, wishing she could reach his hand from where she was sitting. 'Please be all right.'

Suddenly the tears she had been holding back came pouring down her cheeks.

After what seemed an eternity the ambulance slowed to a stop and the doors were flung open. People in scrubs gathered round the stretcher and wheeled it fast through the double doors while the paramedic called out incomprehensible figures.

'Leave them to it,' said a nurse as Elsie tried to follow them into a room with bright lights and a lot of shiny equipment. 'You can sit here while you wait. We'll need to look you over. Do you know him?'

'He... he... he's my boyfriend,' she stuttered.

'Has he any family?'

'Yes.'

'Can you give them the details at the desk?'

Elsie tried to stand, shook like a leaf and collapsed back on to the chair.

'Never mind, you can tell me. Then I'll get you checked out.'

'He tried to kill him!' she burst out. 'He tried to kill my Ken! He will be all right, won't he?'

The nurse put her arm round her as the tears started again, until eventually Elsie was able to give her Ken's name and address.

'But I can't remember the phone number,' she said. 'His father will be at work, but his mother will be at home.'

She looked up and managed a wan smile at the approaching figure.

'Here's Donald,' she said to the nurse. 'I'll be all right now thank-you.'

'Quick,' he said, rummaging in a carrier bag. 'Change your boots. Put your trainers on instead. If you kicked that chap hard with those boots on it will show. You could have even broken his leg. So put these on and hope they don't ask questions. They'll probably think he hit his leg on a rock when he fell.'

'I really don't like all this,' said Elsie. 'I'm not a good liar.'

'You don't have to lie, just don't tell them everything,' said Donald. 'If they ask if you kicked him, say everything happened so fast all you can remember is running at him. If they ask if you've changed your shoes, tell them the truth.'

He put the boots in the bag.

'I'll be back in a minute,' he said. 'I've got your rucksack in the car. Anything you want from it?'

'No,' she said. 'Not yet anyway. I'd just like to make sure Ken is all right. They do seem to be taking a long time.'

'They need to be sure,' Donald said, taking her hand. 'He'll be fine, you'll see.'

Suddenly the doors opened and a trolley was wheeled out fast.

'Where are you taking him?' cried Elsie.

'Just for a CT scan,' reassured the nurse. 'We are concerned that he hasn't regained consciousness yet and we want to make sure he's not bleeding inside his head.'

'You mean his brain? It could be damaged?'

'It's a possibility, but even if it is bleeding the damage isn't necessarily permanent.'

Elsie put her head in her hands. Ken had explained what that man Barnes was after but if she hadn't been there would he have attacked him? Or would Ken have not been distracted by her and heard his attacker soon enough to defend himself? The tree falling on the hut, the body in the walnut tree, and now Ken; she was bad luck. She should have stuck to her guns when she broke it off.

'What's going on?'

She looked up.

'Mrs Bradshaw. Ken was attacked by a man. He was hit on the head with a brick. He's still unconscious.'

'Where is he?'

168

'They've taken him for a scan. They're worried about his brain.'

'It's you, isn't it?' she snapped. 'First my daughter, now because of you I'm going to lose my son as well. Why couldn't you have stayed out of our lives?'

She turned to a nurse.

'I want to see my son,' she said. 'Now.'

'He's getting a CT scan so I'm afraid you'll have to wait. He shouldn't be long. Are you family?'

'Yes, I'm his mother. She's not. I want her out of here.'

The nurse looked stunned.

'But she came in with him.'

Ken's mother stared at the nurse.

'It's all right,' Elsie said. 'I don't want to cause any trouble, I'll go. I have to give a statement to the police anyway, I'll do that somewhere else.'

As she unsteadily got to her feet Donald returned, together with a police officer.

'What's going on?' asked Donald.

Elsie just shook her head.

'I'll make that statement now,' she said wearily to the policeman.

'Can I accompany her?'

'I'd prefer not. You were also a witness. Just procedure.'

'I'll stay here then, if I may Mrs Bradshaw?'

Ken's mother shrugged her shoulders.

Once they got to the waiting area Elsie repeated the story as suggested by Donald.

'Well it's all very clear-cut,' he said. 'Someone of your size could hardly have pushed him over the edge, especially when he had a brick in his hand.'

He glanced at Elsie's shoes.

'He had a nasty gash on his leg. Must have hit it on a rock as he fell.'

Did she imagine the slight smile on his face?

'Now you say the deceased was someone who had been stalking you before this?'

'Yes, I think so,' said Elsie.

'Are you up to identifying him?'

169

She shuddered.

'We can leave it until later?'

'No,' she said. 'I'd prefer to get it over with.'

He walked with her to the mortuary.

'All I can remember is his face all twisted with hate,' she said. 'And that hand with the rock in it, ready to come down on Ken's head again.'

They reached the mortuary and he opened the door.

'Oh dear,' he said, shutting it again. 'They haven't covered him yet.'

'That's OK,' she said. 'Can we do it anyway? There's something else I'd like to look at.'

He led her to the table.

His face, no longer spiteful and bitter, looked pitiable now. She felt sorry for him. What could lead someone to do something like this? What could fill someone with so much hate?

'That's him,' she said. 'That's the man who was following us. And that is the hand that was holding the brick, the hand that was going to kill him.'

'Thank-you,' he said. 'You've done very well. And you saved that other chap's life, from what I hear. Not many people get that chance. I'll take you back to the resuscitation room.'

'No, the waiting area will be fine. His mother doesn't want me there.'

'What? But – '

'No, I've had enough trouble today.'

Shaking his head, the policeman took her back to the waiting area.

Sitting there, she thought for a moment then, taking a deep breath, took out her notebook and pencil and started to write.

22

Darling Elsie,
I admit I cried when my mother gave me your letter. Perhaps it
was the blow on the head, I don't know. I've been so selfish,
knowing the pressures you have been under. I'll love you always
though.
Ken

'I knew no good would come of it,' Elsie's father said. 'Didn't I
say so Mary?'

'Yes dear, you did say so.'

'And was I right?'

'No you weren't right,' snapped Elsie. 'According to the
papers I saved Gordon's life in the hut, and I certainly stopped
that horrible man from killing Ken. So something good did come
of it. Perhaps that's why we met. Now it's over. For ever this
time.'

'Right, so something good came of it for other people, but
what about you? What good did it do you?'

'It made me feel better about myself. Not useless, wasting my
time travelling through my life with nothing to show at the end of
it.'

'That's not fair dear,' said her mother. 'Most people live
normal lives doing normal things and enjoying what they can.'

'Well I wanted to be something different, and for a little while
I thought I could.'

'There you are, it's just upset you,' said her father.

'It's been almost a week,' said her mother. 'Have you heard
how he is?'

'One of the volunteers rang to say he was coming out of
hospital yesterday and doesn't seem to have suffered any long-
term damage.'

Mr Clark turned his head back to the television and Mrs Clark
clicked away at her knitting.

Elsie got up and went to the kitchen to make a cup of tea,
changed her mind and went upstairs to her bedroom. She stroked
the rucksack he had bought her, and rubbed the already clean

171

boots. Her throat started to close up and her eyes began to water. God how she missed him; how she missed all of them. A week ago she'd been a volunteer at Warley Place and promised to the man of her dreams. Six days later, on a dreary Sunday, she was back where she started, promised to no one and not part of that friendly lot of eccentrics.

Cheer up, they'd said at work when she told them she'd broken it off; plenty more fish in the sea. But there weren't, not for her.

The door bell rang. She looked at her watch. Three o'clock on a Sunday afternoon. Probably Jehovah's Witnesses. She heard a woman's voice, quiet at first, then raised. It sounded like Ken's mother, and it sounded like her own mother was on the receiving end. She went to her door to listen. No, it wasn't fair, it wasn't her mother's fault, what she had done. She opened the door and went down the stairs.

'Elsie,' said Mrs Bradshaw. 'I've come to apologise for what I said to you in the hospital. I've no excuses. I was worried about Ken and wanted to blame someone. You were handy. It was unforgivable of me.'

'No, you were right,' said Elsie. 'I've brought nothing but bad luck to him. I love him and always will, but he can do better.'

'No 'e can't,' came a voice from the other room.

'Your father's right,' said Mrs Bradshaw. 'He couldn't do better. I want to ask you a big favour.'

'What's that?'

'Come back with me. Now. Ken is as miserable as sin. Donald has told me how you saved his life at some peril to your own, attacking a violent man like that, a slip of a girl like you. That was a very brave thing to do. Ken told me he asked you to marry him. I'd like that. I'd like it very much indeed. Please come.'

'Go on girl,' called her father.

'Go on,' said her mother.

'I'll get my coat,' said Elsie.

'She's made all the difference to Ken,' Elsie heard Mrs Bradshaw say. 'We lost our Marion you know, and I get a bit possessive of him. I'm frightened of losing him too. But Elsie will take care of him as well as I can. Better.'

'Elsie thinks the world of him. It's changed her life, for sure.'

172

Elsie slipped on her anorak and came downstairs.

'I really am sorry,' said Mrs Bradshaw when they were in the car. 'I don't know what came over me.'

'Don't worry about it. I really do understand. I was thinking the same thing myself. How is he? Will he be OK? They said he probably would.'

'He's fine. He mustn't drive for a few days and he's got a headache, but he's going to be none the worse for it in a week or so. He'll be a lot better for seeing you. He doesn't know I came for you by the way. He thought perhaps you'd had enough.'

'Me? Had enough? Never!'

'Did you really go for Barnes as Donald said?'

'Well I'm not supposed to say.'

'Donald explained that. But he said you threw yourself at him and kicked him in the shins.'

'Yes, and those boots have very hard toe caps. His shin made a funny noise. I think it might have broken. But you'd have done the same. It wasn't brave, it was just a reaction.'

'Did Ken tell you about Barnes?'

'Yes. I don't believe what he said. Barnes, that is, not Ken.'

'Well there have been rumours about someone stealing Miss Willmott's plants about that time.'

'I still don't believe it.'

She steered the car into their drive and sat still.

'Go on,' she said. 'Go and ring the bell.'

'I'm nervous,' said Elsie. 'A bit shy.'

'Go on, for goodness sake.'

Elsie got out and walked to the door; the door she never thought she'd see again. She pressed the illuminated button.

There were footsteps and the door opened. His miserable face lit up like the sky as a thundercloud clears from the sun.

'Elsie!' he cried.

She threw herself into his arms, arms that wrapped themselves round her as he almost carried her into the lounge. They kissed a long, long kiss.

'I've heard what you did to that fellow,' he said eventually. 'How can I ever thank you? How can I ever say sorry for getting you into that position?'

'Ken, stop apologising and thanking me,' she laughed delightedly. 'Oh I've missed you.'

'Why didn't you come?'

'I thought I'd brought you such bad luck you'd be better off without me.'

'It's my fault,' said his mother, coming into the room. 'I was nasty to her. I said some things.'

'Nothing I wasn't thinking myself,' said Elsie.

'Hello Elsie,' said Ken's father, coming in from the garden and giving her a hug. 'Lovely to see you again.'

'Tea?' asked Mrs Bradshaw. 'And cakes?'

'Yes please to both,' said Elsie, still clinging to Ken's hand and letting go only to sit down next to him.

'What's happened about that body we found in the walnut tree?' Elsie asked.

'Oh, apparently someone went missing in 1920 and the police said he was a well known petty thief. There was also talk of him thieving from Warley Place, but they never managed to prove that. How on earth he ended up concreted in the walnut tree we'll never know.'

'Perhaps Ellen Willmott caught him,' laughed Ken. 'She'd soon have him concreted safely away!'

'Actually they did wonder at the time if she'd caught him stealing her plants,' said Ken. 'She was away at the time of his disappearance though.'

'Well I do know something,' said Elsie, pulling her now dog-eared notebook from her pocket. 'See that hand?' She pointed to her sketch of the concrete with a skeletal hand protruding from it. 'See his little finger is deformed?'

'Yes,' said Ken, puzzled.

'Well that man Barnes that tried to kill you has the same crooked finger. I saw it when he was holding the brick but I thought I might have imagined it so I checked in the hospital and it's exactly the same. I bet the thief was one of his ancestors.'

'If so, it means that Barnes was related to him,' said Ken turning to his father. 'So rather than your grandfather starting your business by stealing plants, it was Barnes' grandfather that was the thief. I wonder if we could get a DNA check done?'

'No,' said his father. 'Best just leave it. Unless his family want to make something of it, then we can tell them what we know. That will shut them up. I think that will be the end of any rumours about our dubious origins.'

'I wonder if your grandfather was the one who concreted him,' said Ken. 'Perhaps he found him stealing and killed him in a fight, didn't know what to do with the body so put it in there.'

'You do think up some daft tales,' said his mother. 'Oh, wasn't there something else, Stephen?'

Elsie's face fell. This was where they said thank-you very much and goodbye.

'No, it's good,' Ken's father said hurriedly. 'At least, I think it is. It's about Morelands.'

'I thought we were letting that go?' said Ken, then explaining to Elsie. 'Morelands was a small nursery a little way off the main roads. It's where we started, where young Alfie Hedges had his first nursery. The trouble is it's not easy to expand and wouldn't get any passing trade. There's a little cottage there and it's got a bit overgrown now.'

'I've had second thoughts,' Ken's father continued. 'I thought we'd get a small specialist nursery going. No books, no fancy gift shop, no trays of pansies and geraniums. Just plants that are a bit different. Something I've been thinking about for ages, but haven't really had the time.'

'Are you saying what I think you're saying?' asked Ken, his eyes widening and a grin spreading across his face.

'Yes I am. You and Elsie. A bit of help from your mum and me to begin with, but it would be your baby. We'd get the cottage done up a bit. It would be somewhere for you to live and you could keep an eye on the place too. Elsie could prepare a really fancy brochure. Those sketches of yours, Elsie, they're really good. It's would be far better than the usual load of boring photographs. I bet in a few years it would be a collector's item.'

Elsie's jaw dropped. 'But I'm not that good.'

'You are, and you'll be even better when you've been to art classes.'

'But I don't have the time or the money. I work most evenings.'

'You'll have the time if you work for me. And I'll pay for the classes. It's a business expense, an investment.'

'I don't know what to say.'

'Yes, will do.'

'Well yes, I can't believe it. I won't let you down.' She turned to Ken, bubbling over with enthusiasm. 'We could grow some of Ellen Willmott's plants if we can track them down, couldn't we? And perhaps grow some Warley Place trees from their seed? They wouldn't mind, would they? And – '

'Hold your horses,' laughed Ken. 'It's not that big and there will be lots of work to do before we sell anything.'

'When can we see it?'

Ken looked at his father.

'Go on, she'll never eat her tea if she doesn't see it first,' he said. 'See you back here about six. Just be careful, you shouldn't really be driving.'

'That magnolia in the walled garden with the big leaves,' Elsie continued as Ken grabbed her hand and led her out to his car. 'Perhaps we could get some of those growing...'

Her mind was buzzing with ideas and she hardly noticed where they were going until they pulled up in front of a large padlocked wooden gate. Ken got out and unlocked it and they drove up the short path to the cottage.

'I'm sorry about the state it's in,' he said. 'But – '

'Ken it's lovely,' she broke in. It was indeed in a pretty poor state. Once a lovely little bungalow with an open porch and leaded glass windows, little work had been done on it since the Bradshaws decided to sell the site; but Elsie could see in her mind's eye already the perfect home with hanging baskets and flowers growing each side of the front door. The large garden, full of weeds and overgrown paths, was a thriving nursery packed with exotic plants. There was a large shed that could be converted into a place to deal with customers and a rather tatty greenhouse that would have to be enlarged.

As Ken went over to inspect the front door of the bungalow, Elsie, her heart bursting with happiness, wandered round the back of the greenhouse. She glanced down and saw something metallic in amongst the weeds, and bending down and easing them back saw a little oval label. Pulling it out the inscription 'S, WT, 14' appeared embossed on it, just readable through the dirt; an Ellen Willmott label. She glanced across at Ken, grinning from ear to ear as he tried the front door. She gently rubbed the earth away from the lettering and as she held it in her hand she felt a warm contentment in her heart. She slipped it in her bag to return it to its home at Warley Place.

Appendix 1
Bibliography

Books

Miss Willmott of Warley Place by Audrey le Lievre.
This book is no longer in print but is available from the public library and is well worth reading. It provided much of the background information for *The Wall* and *The Walnut Tree*. A computer generated version may be available late in 2008.

Warley Magna to Great Warley by George Harper.
This book is also an excellent reference source, both for Warley Place and for the wider history of the locality. It is also available in the public library.

Warley Place
This well illustrated Essex Wildlife Trust booklet is an excellent guide to the people, the fauna and the flora of Warley Place.

The Wall
The Walnut Tree is a sequel to this previous novel and although it can be read without reference to its predecessor, some references to previous events do occur.

Websites

http://www.essexwt.org.uk/main/welcome.htm
This is the website of Essex Wildlife Trust. As well as providing information on all the EWT nature reserves and on wildlife in general it provides the information to enable you to become a member. Alternatively just ring 01621 862960 or call in at one of the visitor centres.

http://www.warleyplace.org.uk

This is the Warley Place website, set up in December 2007. Here you will find photographs and regularly updated information on events at the reserve.

http://www.spetchleygardens.co.uk/

Spetchley Park, near Worcester, was and is the home of the Berkeley family into which Rose Willmott, Ellen's sister, married. The gardens still exist and are well worth a visit.

Appendix 2
Biographies

Ellen Willmott
Ellen Ann Willmott was born in 1858 and with her father, mother and sister Rose, moved to Warley Place in 1875. She had always had a keen interest in gardening and following the death of her parents and the marriage of her sister (later, sadly, also her death) she ran the estate on her own.

She was a very wealthy woman, her money partly handed down from her own father and partly given to her by her godmother.

She had many interests apart from gardening. She had some very expensive musical instruments and was a good violinist and choral singer. She was a photographer and her book *Warley Place in Spring and Summer* (which can be viewed in Brentwood Library) contains a number of her photographs. She also had her own lathe, printing press and telescope. But it was gardening that was her overriding passion and she developed a garden that was second to none.

Although the First World War did not help matters, the truth is that she spent too much money both on Warley Place and her estates in Italy and France. By the end of the war she struggled from one financial crisis to the next and her death in 1934 mercifully happened before she would finally have had to sell Warley Place.

She was a remarkable woman.

James Robinson
James Robinson started work for the Willmott family in 1890 and served until Ellen Willmott's death. He developed from the butler to someone who ran the house and became her confidant. He was rewarded by the gift of The Red House in which he was able to live out what few years he had left.

Jacob Maurer
Ellen Willmott 'poached' Jacob Maurer from his Swiss employer in 1894. He was a quiet man, liked and respected by all who knew

him, and dedicated to the development of the Alpine Garden, although as things became more difficult and the number of gardeners diminished he had to spread his energies a little further.

He lived in South Lodge, eventually, with his wife Rosina and nine children. When you look at South Lodge you wonder how they were all squeezed in!   Sadly his wife died in 1918 of tuberculosis. He later married Maggie Saywood, whose mother ran the bothy in which he stayed before he married Rosina.

He stayed at Warley Place until it was sold on Ellen Willmott's death, then moved to Gidea Park (not Billericay, as wrongly stated in *The Wall* and in *Miss Willmott of Warley Place*) to stay with his son John. He then moved back to his native Switzerland and died in 1937.

Appendix 3
Warley Place as it is now

This map and the accompanying notes, from which the events related in the book can be located, have been taken from the Essex Wildlife Trust Warley Place Trail Guide, suitably abbreviated to suit the text.

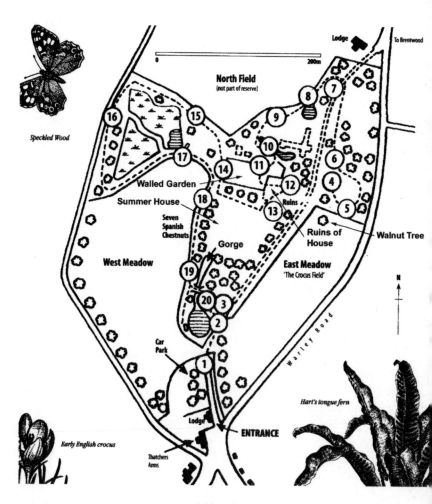

The aim of the Trust at Warley Place is to improve the different habitats for the benefit of the wildlife while retaining those parts of the garden that have survived.

Warley Place is open to members of Essex Wildlife Trust or to other members of the public by appointment. Please keep to the footpaths. Some parts of the reserve are dangerous because of hidden cellars and decaying walls.

The numbers below are those appearing on the marker posts on the walk round the reserve.

1. On the left as you enter the gate is the old lodge in which Jacob Maurer and his family lived. The drive from the gate to the car park borders the crocus field (East Meadow), which, in spring, used to be a sea of purple flowers. Some crocuses can still be seen in the field and in the border to the drive, but most do not now flower, apparently because of grazing by rabbits. This is one of the few sites in Britain where the early English crocus grows naturally.

2. The South Pond is all that remains of the medieval water point for Great Warley village. The main coloniser is common reed, but yellow flag and marsh marigold are among other water plants. The path from the car park to the stile and on through the reserve was the drive to the house and before that the main road from Great Warley to Brentwood. The road was moved to its present position in the 19th century.

3. In late winter, snowdrops of many varieties can be seen bordering the path. Near the top of the slope, on the left, is where the house stood until it was demolished in 1939; the turning circle is still visible. Opposite, on the right, a ha-ha borders the crocus field. The ditch and wall kept grazing cattle out of the garden without the need for a hedge, which would have blocked the view. In the meadow stands the walnut tree dating from Ellen Willmott's time.

4. Notice the remains of the coach house on the left. There is a barrier across the old drive here and two smaller paths lead off to the right through the old orchard area and rockery. Beyond the barrier is 'the butterfly ride', an open area with flowering shrubs and nettles to attract butterflies. Taking the path to the right leads through a patch of Abraham, Isaac and Jacob *Trachystemon orientalis*, another relic of Miss Willmott's time.

5. In spring and summer the characteristic smell of onions at this point indicates ransoms or wild garlic which is well established. Other plants include *Corydalis*, hart's tongue ferns and meadow saffron.

6. This area was recently cleared of bamboo and bramble. The large tree on the right is a Tree of Heaven *Ailanthus*.

7. This was the main cold frame area of the garden. Following the removal of sycamores and ivy, many attractive flowers appear each year.

8. The artificial pond was a reservoir for watering the cold frames and greenhouses. The site of the group of greenhouses can be seen from the plan attached to the rail.

9. The ivy-covered stump on the right was a sycamore that lived for about 140 years. It was used as a resting point for tawny owls until the top fell off.

10. Next to the nursery is a narrow half-moon shaped pond and beyond it a brick-sided reservoir similar to the one at post 8.

11. The walled garden probably dates from the 17th century, but much of it is the result of Miss Willmott's planting. There is a fine ginkgo tree, a few magnolias and a palm. A considerable amount of work is being done to repair the wall which in places was in poor condition.

12. The house was demolished in 1939 and much of the ground floor has fallen into the cellars. Mosaic flooring can be seen in

places. The small building now used as an information room and a tea-room for volunteers was a cloakroom and WC. A variety of ferns flourish in the cellar.

13. The conservatory was part of the house and still stands, though without a roof or glazing. Its mosaic floor is raised so that tepid water could be stored beneath. The large window leads out to what was the lawn and bowling green. The building was in a dangerous condition but has recently been stabilised to make it safe for people to enter.

14. From the terrace, which is currently being restored, there was a clear view of the lakes at the bottom of the slope.

15. Bluebells can be seen on the left and the two large trees on the right are a large turkey oak and a Caucasian wing-nut.

16. The lower tree-covered area was the bog garden and a concrete-edged boating lake. The lake floor now hardly shows so much as a puddle, even in the wettest weather. At the far end there is the wall of the old boat house with a rail still in position.

17. The hide overlooks the North Pond, which is reputed to have been a carp pond when the estate belonged to the nuns of Barking Abbey.

18. The Spanish or sweet chestnuts were reputed to have been planted by the diarist John Evelyn in the 17th century. On the left is the partly restored old summer house.

19. The large beech tree on the left was planted about 1810, but the top had to be cut off to render it safe. Along the spur to the hide overlooking South Pond can be seen patches of purple toothwort.

20. The bridge spans the gorge which Miss Willmott had constructed as part of her Alpine Garden. The rocks were brought from Yorkshire. The remains of the filmy fern cave can be seen from here.

Appendix 4
Warley Place as it was

This map of Warley Place was taken and adapted from the booklet *Warley Place* with kind permission of the Essex Wildlife Trust. It actually relates to the year 1904 but should be sufficient for the purposes of this book.

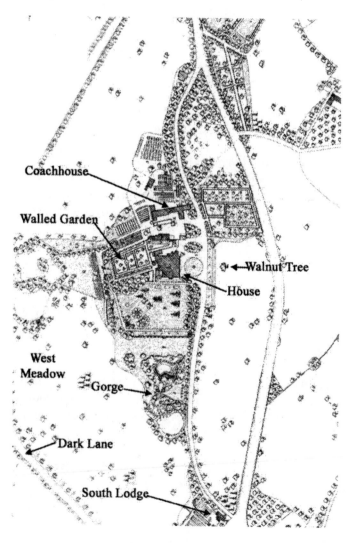

Appendix 5
Warley Place – The House

This plan of the house as it was during Ellen Willmott's time was taken from the Essex Wildlife Trust booklet *Warley Place*.

The house was demolished in 1938 or 1939 partly because it had deteriorated to the extent that it was becoming dangerous and partly to make room for a proposed development that never took place.

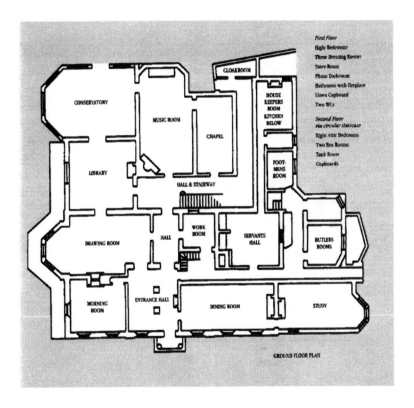

187

Appendix 6
Spetchley Park

This layout of Spetchley Park, the home of the Berkeley family and Rose Berkeley, Ellen Willmott's sister, has not changed greatly over the years and may be of use in tracing the sisters' walk described in chapter 7.

The events described in this chapter are as fictitious as the rest of the book, but Ellen Willmott did indeed travel to Spetchley Park on a number of occasions and worked with her sister to develop the gardens as a whole and the Fountain Gardens in particular.

Although, unlike Warley Place, toilets and tea rooms are provided, the gardens themselves still exude an atmosphere of peace and tranquillity in which one can escape from the nonsense noises of modern life.

They cover about 30 acres and contain many rare and beautiful plants. Located near Worcester, they are well worth a visit.

At the time of writing opening times are 11 to 6, Wednesday to Sunday, from 21 March to 30 Sept and Bank Holiday Monday, and on Saturdays and Sundays in October from 11 to 4.

Check on the website www.spetchleygardens.co.uk for further information.

2	Horse Pool
3	West Border
4	Millennium Garden
5	South Border
7	Fountain Gardens
9	Conservatory
17	The Long walk
18	The House

The above image does not do justice to the Spetchley Park gardens but serves as a guide to Ellen Willmott and Rose Berkeley's walk in chapter 7.

You are probably already a member of Essex Wildlife Trust, but if you are not have you considered joining?

EWT has 7 Visitor Centres, 87 Nature Reserves, and manages over 7,000 acres of land. It is very active in teaching children and adults in matters relating to nature and conservation – almost 40,000 of them last year at well over 1,000 separate events.

To find out more either look at the website (www.essexwt.org.uk) or drop in at one of the visitor centres at Abberton Reservoir, Bedford's Park, Chafford Gorges, Fingringhoe Wick, Hanningfield Reservoir, Langdon (Plotlands) or Thorndon Country Park.

Alternatively ring 01621 862960 and information will be posted to you.